PUGET SOUND

fifteen stories

C.C. Long

PLEASURE BOAT STUDIO

A Literary Press

Puget Sound: 15 Stories
By C.C. Long
Copyright © 2005

 Published by Pleasure Boat Studio: A Literary Press, 201 W.89th Street, #6F, New York, NY 10024 , Tel 212.362.8563, Fax 888.810.5308, e-mail pleasboat@nyc.rr.com, URL www.pbstudio.com

Long, C.C.

Puget Sound: 15 Stories / C.C. Long

ISBN 1-929355-22-X

First printing

*Design and Composition
by Francis P. Floro*

Library of Congress
Cataloging-in-Publication
Data

Long, C. C. (Charles C.)
Puget Sound : 15 stories
/ C.C. Long. p. cm.
ISBN 1-929355-22-X (alk. paper)
1. Puget Sound Region (Wash.)
—Fiction. 2. Washington (State)
—Social life and customs—Fiction.
I. Title. PS3612.O49P84 2005
813'.6--dc22   2004025115

For Rebecca, Isabel, Thelma and Mark
with special thanks to Peter Stewart

CONTENTS

Puget Sound 7

Prayers and Cancer and Bombs 17

How to Make a Totem Pole 23

Turkey Shoot 31

Whale Tale 37

Missing Link 49

Falling from the Sky 59

A Story Not to Be Believed 75

A Story of Rape 89

Grunge Redux 95

Tommy Baseball 105

Sacred Salmon 111

Between the Mad and the Mundane 123

Space Needle 133

Deception Pass Bridge 139

PUGET SOUND

William Hauser, also known as Willie and Wham-bam, now the only remaining member of the rock-and-roll band of the ages, *Puget Sound*, a band that never played together except on this beach two months before this gray morning, looks out at Penn Cove where a pod of killer whales circle in sea-weed-green cold waters, gulping down smelt, lapping up the bounty of the freakish appearance of a mass gathering of the silvery fish that come to lay their eggs on the gravelly beaches of the cove and are often raked up by avid smelt men who use wire mesh rakes and haul huge bounties of the succulent sardines out of the brine. The whales breach, flying in frenetic rhythm, the water not able to hold their enthusiasm for the smorgasbord, and land in a resounding body flop that echoes over the calm water.

The day is varying degrees of gray, the only color there is in the universe on this foggy September morning. The water rolls in and out, unleashing a rock-and-rolling schism of percussion that dulls the senses. Willie Hauser walks into the water in his Nike hiking shoes up to his ankles. The coldness makes him tingle. He is six foot two, lean; his short-cropped hair is black but shows traces of the blond that he had dyed it months ago. His beard is a stubbly dark shadow, a sign of not shaving for two days. He looks down and sees the smelt circling his tattooed ankles. He kicks them away and then walks back to the driftwood where his sleeping bag and duffle lie as proof of his night of passing out on the beach. People are looking for him. People are dead. He is in deep.

He sits and lights his Camel. What is his next move? He has to get the hell out of here but he has no money, no car, nothing, except the duffle bag with that magical artifact that had led him to where he is now. Gill dead. Danny dead. Puget Sound dead. And himself ready to die. Make that deadly artifact. How did he get to this point, to this place where it all began? Three twenty-year-old drop outs just laid off by the Useless Bay Marina with no real clue now or ever, lamenting, beer drunk, taking pisses in the cove. Gill with his acoustic guitar, Danny with his harmonica, and him with his sticks, beating on a can while Gill fingered an Oasis tune and Danny sang like a vintage rocker. They decided they'd start a band and call it Puget Sound. It was better than joining the army and getting killed in Iraq. They celebrated their decision by dancing in the lapping waves of the full-moonlit cove. That's when they saw something shimmering in the water.

They had all thought it was a silver salmon until Danny stepped forward and pulled the glimmer from the cold salty water. They fell back in awe as he raised it up and the face came into view, glittering gold, green and blue, intricate and old but not showing its age. They thought at first it was a mascot's mask for the Seattle Seahawks, but when they got back to Gillis' car, they realized it might be valuable. It looked like real gold with inlaid emeralds; but instead of taking it seriously, they just got drunker and headed into Coupeville and wore the mask around town like morons. They drank more and ended up at the Captain Whidbey Bar wearing the mask and dancing around like crazy cats.

That's where it started to go wrong. Lyle the bartender had called them over and told them that they might think about calming down before he had to throw them and their mask out. Then he asked to see the mask. He took a look and shook his head. "You dip shits better take care of this thing. It might be worth some money."

They thanked him and flippantly yowled that of course it was worth something, and they were all going to be millionaires, rock-and-roll star millionaires!

In the corner unnoticed by them were a couple guys drinking whiskey and watching their antics. The whole world could know for all they cared; they were clueless about the mask's worth and about what ends some folk might go to get their hands on it. Hell, they didn't care; they were lost in delusions of limos, mansions, and all the cable TV you could watch, not to mention women by the truckload and booze that would fill lakes. They had hit the mother lode.

Then one of the strangers walked over and asked if he could look at the mask. After a quick inspection he offered them a hundred dollars for it. In their drunkenness they almost sold it right there and then, and if they had maybe none of this would have happened.

William smokes another butt, trying to figure out his next move. He has to get this mask back to Dr. Seymour at the University of Washington. Dr. Seymour would take care of it. He was the expert who had said that the mask was authentic and one of a kind. It was especially intriguing because the Northwest Indian tribes that had practiced shamanism had no access to gold and emeralds; this being the case it served up a lot of questions and might be a holy grail piece in the antiquities of the early Haida Tribe of Vancouver Island.

Dr. Seymour had also told them that the mask was surely treasured and magical, that it held mystical secrets of the ancient Haida. He begged them to leave it with him, but they had refused. As they left he mentioned that the mask might bring the carrier some bad luck. They laughed.

Soon after that, Gillis' car's brakes went out on Highway 20 and he went head on into a tree, killing himself. A day later Danny ended up dying in his shower, slipping on soap and crushing his skull on enamel. Both of the deaths looked like they were without fault and blame, just a part of the mundane tragedy of life. But Willie knew better: it was no curse; it was the strangers. He had noticed them a couple of times following him. He had reported it to the Island County Sheriff's office but was given no regard. His word didn't hold a lot of water in these parts. His past of petty crimes and lies had caught up with him. He checks under the bag to make sure it is there. It has a hold on him. The gold and emeralds sparkling and shining. It is polished and magical. Seagulls pick up clams and drop them on the rocks around him and then swoop down and gulp the salty contents. He is hungry but not that hungry. He never had a taste for raw clams. He lights another cigarette and presses his back against the log feeling the hardness. He wants to sell the mask but has no clue where to find buyers. He would even sell it to the diabolical strangers if they made themselves known.

He had thought about prying the emeralds and gold from the icon and selling them, but even in desperation and with a past that had been filled with participating in worse criminal antics than defacing antiquities, he could not bring himself to destroy the mask. He realized his only choice in this debacle was to give the mask to the Professor and see what he could get for it. He blows smoke rings. There is not going to be a million-dollar payday: he isn't going to be a rock-and-roll star, but he might be able to save his skin.

He thinks about his dead friends, feels suddenly feint, tosses his cig into the green sea and walks back to his sleeping bag and pulls the mask out of the bag again. He touches the mask, puts it on his face and looks around only to find himself staring at a black Caddie driving up Highway 20 across the cove from him. He pulls the mask off and puts it in the bag quickly, nervously, fearfully, and runs with it up the beach to where he knows a rowboat is tied up.

He places the mask in the boat and jumps in as he sees the car screeches to a stop and two thugs jump out pulling out guns, running clumsily down the beach. He rows with all his might, whimpering in fear, heading for the pod of killer whales; and he ducks as he hears two shots fly over his head.

He sees the bullets plunk into the water near the whales. He yells to them that he would sell them the mask but they don't hear him. He watches as the men look out at him, now too far away to shoot. He lifts the mask in their direction and threatens to drop it in the water, right back where it came from. The men wave frantically and then start to run back to their car. He puts down the oars and watches.

He notices that around him the pod of killer whales circle his small boat, slowly. They do not threaten him. They seem just to be curious, making a fusion of squeaks and grunts. They are beautiful. Black with snowy white patches shining in the translucence of the water. Two adults and two pups. They hypnotize him in their circling hydro-dance and call.

He lies back with the mask on his chest and feels the shallow waves of the whales that circle. This slow ebbing and flowing and rock-a-bye-babying makes him sleepy. He closes his eyes and falls into a murky somnolence that is not quite sleep but more like mesmerization.

Willie feels as though he is going down slowly in a maelstrom of a whirlpool being pulled under the water by the circling of the whales. He tries to wake from the trance but can not and instead is brought into a watery world in a timeless history. He is on a canoe of Northwest Indians, rowing through inky moonlit salt water toward a large gathering of other Indians. The sound of laughing, singing, chanting carry across the water and one of his fellow rowers lets out a whoop that startles him and quickens the pace of the canoe. He focuses on the bonfire that sends sparks floating into the eternal ether of the night. He is an Indian going to join the potlatch. They row up onto the beach to the bellicose cheers of his brotherhood.

When the greetings settle, a rhythmic drumbeat drowns out and silences the celebration, drawing all the attention to the water. It is a calm, eerie fluid sparkling with moonlight. When all focus is on the hypnotizing watery blackness, out of it breaks—in a cataclysmic splash—a huge creature, water shedding off of it, wearing the mask. It wades through the water and then stands above them. The mask does not seem to be a mask at all but the head of the creature. Willie falls to his knees in awe, as do the rest of the tribe.

The creature—part man, part fish, part bird—then touches all of their heads with some sort of ointment. When it comes to Willie, the creature breathes humid hot breath on him and then touches his forehead; Willie feels the burn of the touch penetrate his being. He screams and feels like he is drowning. He swims in the blackness finally jerking out of his sleep almost tipping over the rowboat as he gasps for air and tries to right himself.

When he finally catches his breath, he hears a motor. He looks in that direction and sees a small motorboat headed toward him from San De Fuca.

He picks up the oars but realizes that trying to get away is useless, and as the boat comes upon him, without thinking he stands, lifts the mask above his head, and in a yell he had never heard himself yell before, throws the mask into the murky waters of Penn Cove. The men on the boat watch and then shoot, barely missing his head. He falls back into the rowboat counting the seconds he has left in his life and hearing the motorboat cut its engine. He hears the men swearing. "Jackass, do you know what you've done! I'm going to kill you."

"You were going to kill me anyway!" Willie yells, slowly lifting his head, ready to die, coming face to face with a gun. The pistol whip that sends him flying back is violent; blood erupts from his nose. He looks up as he sees the man pull the trigger of the gun, but as he does, out of the depths of the water, breaching brine, a killer whale knocks the man from the boat and the bullet jettisons into the water. Simultaneously from all sides the whales slam into the motorboat, tipping it over and causing the other man to fall in, too.

Willie sits up, his face bloody, stunned but reacting quickly, rowing away from the splashing assassins who are being kept busy by the circling killer whales. One of the Orcas, the largest one, leaps out of the water and Willie stares in disbelief. There on its snout lodged on its face is the mask. The whale breaches again, the mask still attached! It is magnificent, the Orca over twenty feet long, black and white, hovering in the air with the gilded emerald laden mask on, seeming like it was a part of it.

Willie watches in amazement remembering his dream and the creature that had walked from the water and anointed him. This is what he is seeing now, and he watches as the masked whale rise again and again from the water.

He continues to row towards land watching the scene, hearing the screaming and swearing of the two thugs holding onto their overturned boat. He watches from land as the whale pod swims out of the cove toward open waters, the largest Orca continuing to leap from the water, mask sparkling on its head. And then they are gone.

Willie washes his bloody face in the salt water and notices the mark on his forehead. It could have been from the pistol whipping but he knew better; it is the anointment. He touches it and feels the impulse of spontaneous fulfillment. A force that he could not fathom had touched him and it had changed him forever. He listens to the still screaming thugs, picks up his sleeping bag and heads for Highway 20. He does not know where he is going or what he will do. He is following a destiny that all humans are privy to but most never realize. A pull toward something greater and more fulfilling, filled with magic and mystery.

He walks to the highway and sticks out his thumb and is picked up by the first car that is going his way.

PRAYERS AND CANCER
AND BOMBS

She sat at the kitchen table, letting her mind wander, looking at the headline on the paper, "Court declares Bush the winner, Gore wins popular vote by a landslide." We're no longer a democracy, she thought, people get what they deserve. It was all criminal. She was tired, up all night working. The Skagit River still and green in her short horizon. Mt. Baker rose up imitating Mt. Fuji against the blue sky, bluer than polished lapis, conjuring heaven. She wondered how it could look so beautiful yet be so defiled, so poisoned, so trespassed on.

The factory, the arsenic spewing pulp mill from hell, was about ten miles away but she could see the three smokestacks like soldiers puffing white smoke. She pounded a pack of generic cigarettes against the table. He used to hate it when she did that. She finally drew a cigarette from the pack and then placed the pack in front of her so it was squared up alongside the black, plastic remote with the red

17

button. It was amazing what you could find on the Internet and how prayers are always answered.

She lit the cigarette with her Bic lighter that was concealed in a silver holder adorned with a silver raven of Northwest Indian design. He had made it for her. She puffed the cigarette to life, enjoying it.

A thread of smoke circled up and out. Billy, the cat, rubbed against her muddy leg and she picked him up and ran her long fingers through the long black hair. Billy purred and then leaped suddenly down to the yellow linoleum floor. His claws made a tapping.

It was about a year ago, he had come through that door whistling a Beatles tune, carrying a bag of groceries and a bottle of Chablis bragging he was going to make his world famous spaghetti. They had Haagen-Dazs Rum Raisin ice cream for dessert. Then at a commercial during a "Cheers" rerun he sighed, took a puff of his cigarette, and said, "Babe, I got cancer."

It hit her like a pin poke, not hurting but slowly spreading until she was exhausted. Her small prayer of not having to tell him answered.

"It's all right though, the doctor says it might not be bad. I gotta go to the hospital tomorrow for some more tests. The factory is paying for it all. It's just lucky we got them or we'd go under for the doctor bills. That's lucky." He spoke it plain, with no emotion, as if he was talking to himself. She listened. He was only forty and she was only thirty-six. They had watched friends go through it. Far too many

18

friends go through it. The whole gray thing. There was a very orderly chain of events before the cancer finished its work. She knew it would be no different for them. She knew she would be sitting here now a year in the future without him. But she didn't know what it would lead her to do. All she could do was pray.

The chemotherapy started. She could remember them sitting on the steps in the back looking at the factory. They would watch the smoke puff up and disappear in the blue. He would say it like a TV set: "Lucky for us for the factory, without them taking care of the medical stuff, could you imagine the burden that would be set upon us."

"Bless us," she said softly, praying. She had it, too, but he didn't know it. She found out a week before when she went to see why they had not been successful at having a baby. She was told she had lymphoma. They told her the only thing she could do was pray and so that is what she had been doing, not for herself to be cured, but for the myriad of everyday wishes she had. And it seemed to be working. She prayed she would live longer than him so she would never have to tell him. She ordered her doctor to tell no one.

He was as bald as a cue ball and nauseous as a sick dog. Chemo doing its damnation. One day, because the smart voters of Washington State had decided that marijuana could be used medicinally, they gave her a pack of medicinal joints for his sickness from the treatments. They had never smoked marijuana before but they found it immediately enjoyable. She smoked with him out of curiosity and

19

just to be with him. She remembered them out on the back porch, very stoned, him saying, "The U.S. Government grows some nice dope." They laughed at that. When they had smoked up the first pack of marijuana cigarettes and then the second pack, she felt too embarrassed to go back so soon to refill the prescription. So she said her prayers.

One day she was at the checkout line down at the Pay Less and her dentist was in line in front of her. The young girl at the cash register had a pair of headsets on and was bobbing to the music, running the magic UPS lines across the computer light. When she had rung up his total, the dentist pulled out his wallet and a neatly rolled joint fell conspicuously to the floor. She noticed it but pretended not to. When she got home she phoned and explained her situation. He invited her over to his house.

"Very exotic," he explained as he put an ounce of green sticky bud in front of her. She offered to pay but he refused her money.

"I was crazy to think that the U.S. Government could have quality anything. That dentist grows some mean pot," he laughed, and coughed. "Want to see an impression of Telly Savalas?" He lifted his cap off his head exposing his baldness. He liked to joke about it. He never seemed down about it. He had even nicknamed the chemotherapy treatments kimosabe. "Got to get my kimosabe," he'd say on the way to the hospital, both of them stoned to the bone.

She often wondered if anybody ever suspected that they smoked so much marijuana. They were stoned all the time.

People would visit and they'd be in their stonedness looking out. No one ever commented. She suspected that people blamed the "cancer situation" for any personality quirks. It was fun being stoned around people who did not suspect. He called their condition "an inside joke."

They became connoisseurs of all that was sensual—music, ice cream, light, laughter. Lighting a joint one early morning, handing it to her, and walking to the stereo in the living room, he put on a Willie Nelson album full blast and came back to bed and they both smoked the joint and listened to Willie sing, ate coffee Haagen-Dazs ice cream and had sex all day. It was the last great day. Soon after that day, he died, coughing blood.

She stood, seeing a lone sea gull reflected the sunlight. It seemed in some ways the longest ten months of her life, in others, the shortest.

His last words were, "The factory will take care of you, and I love you. I will always love you."

They took care of her all right. They took too good of care of her. Especially after she finally reported her cancer. They had even paid for his funeral, including the slick white marble headstone. Many people had come to the funeral, some she did not know, but the condolences were mostly the same, gray and away. She had seen something then, a mask covering so many of their faces. It crawled. She remembered looking around the cemetery and how all the white headstones stuck out like glaring ghosts. She would not be buried there. She did not like them.

She picked up the glass full of the deadly concoction she had created. Enough Valium, Ludes, and Vioxx to kill a horse, with a bit of Doctor Pepper for taste. Her cancer had taken a turn for the worse since he died. That was all right with her. What she was going to do would be considered terrorism by most, but it was truly an act of desperation, even an act of unselfishness, of concern for others who were sure to suffer the same fate. What did she have left? She drank the poison in one gulp, picked up the plastic box she had set next to her cigarettes, and walked back to the porch through the screen door. It slapped shut behind her. She watched the smoke rise from the three smokestacks and recalled her husband's image, his laugh. At that, she pushed the red button on the plastic box; it detonated the bombs that she had spent all night wiring at the factory. She watched the three smokestacks crumble in front of her and heard the explosion and saw the smoke rise. She lifted her eyes to heaven and bowed her head.

HOW TO MAKE
A TOTEM POLE

The world was falling down around us and nobody seemed to notice. It was not just the dot-com world but the whole damn world. I sat in my office playing with my pendulum balls that banged against each other, causing a soothing click that stirred a Pavlovian response making me want to do it more, waiting to be fired, waiting to hear my stock options were worth zilch, waiting for the end of the world.

There was nothing I could do except watch the mice, that I had never noticed before, scuttle between their holes in the state-of-the-art air conditioners that were never turned on in Seattle. I looked out my window at the awesome view that I had taken for granted: Elliott Bay; the Olympic Mountains rising out the placid water, snow still on the peaks; the busy business of the harbor, boats both mammoth and small, churning and sailing down below me; the arriving and departing of jets from Boeing and Sea-Tac airfields leaving calligraphic jet streams; sea gulls, ravens and geese bouncing on the breezes above the harbor. It was the first time I had noticed any of it in months. But there it was, a view that should never be ignored.

Down on the pier some Pacific Northwest Indians were exhibiting their expertise at carving a totem pole, people gathered around watching the skill at which the Indians used their axes, hatches and blades to slowly produce image on top of image from the large log. They worked with speed and veracity, wood chips flying and the group of people watching steadily grew as I watched from above. The Indians definitely enjoyed their work.

I had done a really dumb thing, not the first nor the last dumb thing I will do. This was dumber than dumb but when you're dealing with dumbness the only thing you can do is be dumber because otherwise it's just a bunch of frustration. So that was my law, be dumber than dumb if you're going to be dumb.

'Death and dumbness are all I see.' In fact, those were my exact words at the company meeting that was called to inject some morale into the troops. The troops actually needed an injection of heroin after half the company was fired because of a loss of confidence in tech stocks. We were a dot-com selling outdoor gear on line and we had not made a profit for three years, since our inception. Still until three months ago the stock was worth over a hundred dollars a share and most of the hundred and fifty staff were millionaires from stock options alone. Now the stock was worth about three hundred cents a share, enough to buy toilet paper. Most of the millionaires were bankrupt and fired just in time for the U.S. government to not allow personal bankruptcy declarations. The joke was on us and you couldn't help but feel that most of the world was smirking delightfully at our hard times. We deserved it. As an industry we had been rubbing everyone's face in it for too long. What could we do besides feel sorry for ourselves; nobody else was going feel sorry for us.

So Mork and Ork took a meeting. Espousing a "new agency order" and waving an American flag, they spoke to us like children... like children. These dumb guys, dumber than dumb, were talking dumb things. And the grand finale was a declaration that everything was all right—don't worry, be happy. This, to a group of people who, on a daily basis, watched millions of dollars evaporate. The company was folding; everybody knew that. Why were they lying, and why were they now standing to leave. Why weren't they taking questions? Why ask why?

So I didn't, I just blurted the now infamous words, "All I see is death and dumbness." And then if that was not dumb enough, I continued to furiously attack Mork and Ork over the whole ordeal, denigrating their management skills, their business philosophy and even their sexual prowess. What I said flew from me so effortlessly that I cannot recall all of it. In my delirium I pounded my fist and with a theatrical flare stood and stormed out of the room. Dead, dumb silence followed.

Now I was back in my office clicking my balls wondering when the axe would fall. Nels, the programmer whom I worked with, stuck his head in and said, coyly, "Brave man," and then darted away. Why shouldn't I be brave? I was born in the home of the brave? That started me wondering about the similarities between brave and dumb, but it became too conceptual and I returned to the clicking balls. I had work to do, but I really did not. The only thing I really had to do was to wait for the proverbial other foot to drop. The heat was getting to me. The phone rang.

"You said what needed to be said," Margaret's voice whispered, the only woman who worked there that I ever considered getting butt naked with. "But I wouldn't have said it. I couldn't afford to lose my job. Do you know how bad the market is, how utterly disastrous? I had a friend who lost her job at Amazon and has been looking for six months. Finally after the foreclosure of her co-op she had to take a job in Akron, Ohio."

"Akron?" I burst out laughing and could not stop.

"It's not funny; it's bad out there," she warned.

"It's horrific in here." I kept laughing.

There was a silence and then she lilted, "Good luck."

If it is going to happen, why don't they just get it over with? Why were these clowns torturing me? Because they could. Maybe I should quit, but then I wouldn't be able to collect unemployment. I was no-hero. I had no pride. I felt fortunate for once in my life for being single. My getting fired would hurt nobody but myself. Just me, me, me, me.

Juan, the mailroom man, walked into my office carrying two thin envelopes.

"Whatever happens, just remember you have a life; Mork and Ork just have jobs," Juan said, the lowest man on the totem pole, the wisest in the office, as he handed me the envelopes, my monthly pay check in one of them. I had forgotten today was payday, a usually celebratory occasion.

Suddenly Mork and Ork bumbled in. They wore clown outfits, or was this my imagination? I looked at Juan to see if he noticed. He didn't seem to, just as Mork and Ork did not seem to notice him. They shut the door behind them, apparently not even noticing Juan was there.

"Do you mind if we talk to you?" Mork said, smiling dumbly with big red lips, blackened teeth and bulbous nose, trying to make me laugh.

"Do you mind if they talk to me, Juan?" I asked.

"Juan, Juan, Juan?" Ork tripped over his over-sized clown shoes totally surprised by Juan's presence. He honked his prank horn.

Juan looked at both of them, then at me. He smiled and left, winking at me. Did he see what I saw?

"How can I help you clowns?" I asked, trying to control my sarcasm, and laughter. I had nothing to lose. I started to wrap my mind around these kings in no clothes. Yes, I was to be fired and since I was no longer under their rule, my eyes were opened and my rancor overflowing. They looked at me as if I was supposed to fire myself.

"Yes, well, um, Marty, I think we're going to have to let

you go. It's just not good for morale having you around. We want to start on fresh soil now. I think we're going to have to let you go," Mork repeated, confused, his big floppy ears jiggling.

"You think?" I asked. "Am I or am I not fired?"

"You are fired," Ork stepped in and said forcefully and then honked his horn, "with six months severance. We're sorry but now is the time we need high morale, single mind-edness, and dedication to propel us to the top again."

I whistled the big-top tune and turned and looked at the breathtaking view, again. "Yes you do," I finally said never looking at them again.

They left tripping and hitting each other over the head with giant foam rubber bananas. I was sad, I was ecstatic, I was relieved, I was worried, I was afraid, I was happy, I cried, I laughed, I got drunk, I danced, I packed my office in a slow, fast way. A slow parade of compatriots shuffled by to pay their respect. They all looked as I used to look, fear in their eyes. The mice scrambled to their hole, scared of all the activity; soon they would have my office to themselves. I left death and dumbness via the elevator, no more dot-com millionaire, no more a man with a future. If I had a family I might never have told them and perhaps committed an ingenious suicide so they would get the insurance money. But I did not have a family and I did not have a job. I had nothing, but for some reason as I stepped onto Pike Street the smell of the Puget Sound wafted through me filling me with its bountiful mirth, the Pacific Northwest Indians carving the log into a totem pole echoed from the pier, the smell of fish from the Market torched my olfactory nerves, and a sense of peace gave me relief I had not felt in years.

TURKEY SHOOT

Jenny Boe sat on the step chewing the sleeve of her dress unconsciously. It was an unusually warm December day: a Chinook wind blew. Jenny's hair, blonde and unbrushed, jumped up and down, away from her head. She looked across the farmland that stretched to the bluffs that fell down to the Strait of Juan de Fuca and the mouth of Puget Sound. The grass, brown from the wet weeks that had passed, bent leaning with the wind. A few strands, growing under the steps, brushed the back of Jenny's legs tickling her. The sky was blown blue with whitish pink horsetail-shaped clouds reflecting the light, stretched and broken at the horizon. The sun hung three quarters of the way through its daily journey in the sky.

Jenny could see the grass being blown for miles; past the old barn with holes in the roof; past the mailbox that stood like a tin soldier by the road; past the historic block house that sat beside the road waiting for any driver to stop

31

and inspect its shorn log construction and smell its history; past the rusted, wrecked truck that stuck out of the grass like an animal carcass; down to the bluffs where the Haida Indians so many years ago in vengeance for the killing of one of their own landed their cedar canoes and crawled up to Captain Ebey's house and cut off his head. Jenny had been told that story many times until she could imagine the painted red men crawling over the bluff waiting to attack. The history of the island lived in her view; this was where the first Europeans settled Whidbey Island. The blockhouse was a fortress against Indian incursions.

A small whirlwind caught Jenny's attention; it spun gaily along the dirt path that led from the steps to the gravel driveway. It spun dirt thin at the bottom, thick at the top. The whirlwind died in the gravel, being sucked up by something there.

The wooden screen door slapped loudly behind Jenny, making her jump. She looked back at her mother standing behind the door. She sucked the sleeve of her dress harder. She then turned back to the grass, sky and road. She was waiting for her birthday present from her father. It could be anything. She pressed her knees together. A lone tumbleweed rolled across the tops of the grass and was caught by the mailbox.

Jenny's heart rushed when she saw the pickup truck come into her view in the distance. A black silhouette moving and growing. It moved up the road towards her. Jenny stood and watched as the truck came closer. She could barely hold back her excitement, she wanted to run and meet the truck halfway, to hug it and her daddy together.

James Boe could make out Jenny sitting on the steps. He sighed, knowing she was probably waiting for a horse, or a computer, or some other dream gift. This year, that was an impossibility, as it had been for the preceding five years. So much for the largest economic expansion in history. That expansion had passed him by. High school graduates weren't reaping the rewards of the high-tech economy. Of course there were many things to blame, not least himself. He prepared himself for the salvos that would be aimed at him from his ex-wife when he gave Jenny her present.

Jenny ran to the truck smiling, pushing her head through the window and kissing him on the cheek. She was the only thing he had in his life if you didn't count an overdue bar bill at the tavern and his bung-holed truck.

"What is it?" she asked, looking at he crate in the back of the truck.

"Hold your horses," he said, regretting he even mentioned the word horse. He got out of the truck and carried her to the truck bed. "Take a look," he said.

She slid the wooden spin lock and looked in and felt the sour musk hit her face. She burst out of the box like cannon fire, thrilled by it. "It's a turkey!" she cried.

Her voice made him suddenly happy. Then he looked up to see Mary Boe's silhouette behind the screen door, a snake of smoke crawling from her mouth out from the screen. "Play with it. I'm going talk to your mom."

33

She looked at him smiled and said, "Does it bite?"

"No, it's just a baby," he said, walking off to take his medicine.

Mary Boe watched the most worthless man she had ever met in her life walking toward her. He probably needed to borrow money again. How could she have ever married and had a child with him? But she knew the answer to that often-asked question and it pissed her off. It was the old small-town, stuck-in-the-muck, stay-around, who-do-you-fuck thing. She had married him right out of high school, pregnant as a pig, hoping his captainship of the high school wrestling team might mean a successful future or some other idiot notion like that.

There marriage lasted two years, but really only until she had the baby. After that he was missing in action, downtown bar-flying, fired from numerous jobs. He was a total loser. They lived in a studio apartment in Coupeville for those two years over looking Penn Cove. She tried to forget it all, but you can't in small towns. An inheritance from her grandfather had included the house and about one hundred acres of land that she had been selling in small plots to pay the bills and get by. Here he came, loser of the universe, sauntering up to her, still swaggering like the captain of the wrestling team. It was pathetic. She walked away from the door into the kitchen, retreating.

"Mary." She heard his pathetic voice. "Mary."

"You might as well take that turkey back to Sherman's right now because if you don't it will be soup in the morning," she said with as much disdain as she could conjure. She did not look at him, just lit another cigarette.

"But she loves it." He looked back at Jenny holding the white gawky bird that stood a good foot high already.

She sighed, "Of course she likes it, shit-for-brains. You gave it to her."

He moaned.

"I'm not taking care of a turkey. Turkey's are dirty, dumb birds. I don't have the time or the money to keep a turkey. Get it? Didn't you have any money to just buy her a Barbie? So what did you do, jump over Sherman's fence and steal it?"

He turned away and looked at Jenny. He had been nailed as usual. He couldn't help not having money; he hadn't inherited a farm. "What am I supposed to do? I don't have any money!" he yelled back.

She looked at him disdainfully. "Maybe you should rob a bank?" She sucked the cigarette with a vengeance.

"I thought about it," he said nervously, trying to show his desperation.

"Do it!" she laughed, "Do it! What else are you good for?"

"Come on, Mary. I need some money." He begged like a little boy caught stealing candy trying to get off the hook.

"Get the fuck out of here!"

"Mary," he pleaded hopelessly.

"Did you hear me? Get the fuck out of here and take your lame fucking stolen turkey with you!"

She turned and inhaled most of the rest of the cigarette.

"But it's Jenny's birthday. She loves it. She is my daughter."

Her hair stood on end. There was no escaping that. The club he would use to bludgeon her for the rest of her life. She turned and just stared at him. 'Why can't he just die?' she thought. "She loves it but she's not going to take care of it. She's not going to clean up after it, or feed it, or do any damn thing to it. Get it?"

He looked at her and his anger began to rise. "Jesus Christ, Mary, what do you want me to do, break her heart?"

"What I want you to do is get the fuck out of here and take that lame-ass turkey with you," she yelled, opening the screen door and motioning him to get out.

"Fuck you, Mary," he whimpered, walking through the door powerless.

She watched him walk toward Jenny. She watched Jenny chasing the turkey around the yard, and then she slammed the screen door, mad as hell. She walked directly to her bedroom and pulled out the .22-caliber rifle she kept there. She took it from the case and loaded it with six bullets. She walked with a purpose, blood pumping in her head, stopped at the screen door, opened it slowly, and brought the rifle to her shoulder and aimed through the scope and pulled the trigger without hesitation. The sharp sound of rifle fire stopped all action. She lowered the rifle and heard her daughter cry, but that did not stop her from feeling the power of life and death. She had hit that turkey right between the eyes.

WHALE TALE

He mowed the lawn without thinking, smelling it, grass stains on his high top Nike's. He hurried because it looked like rain. The leaves turned and he knew he didn't have much time so he sped on, back and forth until what lay in front of him was the last strip of lawn. Halfway down it the first drop of rain splattered on the driveway cement. He finished the strip, turned off the motor, took off the bag full of grass and rolled the mower into the garage with one hand, carrying the bag with the other as it started to downpour.

No one was home. He swung the refrigerator door open and checked the contents, taking a dill pickle from a jar. He bit, walked to the living room, and fell into a comfortable chair, leg over its armrest. The rain now fell in a torrid monsoon. He watched through the picture window and listened to its syncopation. His mother and father were gone for the day and night, and it was raining, of course. Vince was on his way but what would they do? He sucked on the pickle and thought about drinking a beer.

Thank God he was getting out of here. Two more weeks and he was on his way to Washington State University in Pullman in Eastern Washington, a veritable desert. He would be a freshman in college, finally. He heard Vince's four-wheel drive pull into the driveway. Vince jumped out of the cab of his truck and ran to the front door, his coat collar pulled up over his head. He swore at the rain all the way to the door. He walked in without knocking.

"Nice day if it doesn't motherfucking rain." He shook himself like a dog. "Ya know you expect rain every other month of the year, but August is supposed to be golden. You know? But uh, shit no, the last August of our existence in this po-dunk town and we get rained on about every motherfucking day." Vince was going to Central Washington University in Ellensburg, another desert town in Eastern Washington.

Tye looked up from his pickle, stared out at the rain, and said with a grin, "Yep."

"What are we going to do, bro?" He reached into his coat pocket and pulled out a bottle of Oly, twisted the top and drank. This would be known for the summer of non- stop partying, a beer always in your pocket and a joint not too far behind.

"Search me." Tye finished the pickle. "Go for a ride?"

"Where to, crew?" Vince closed his eyes tight.

"We could go down to the bowling alley, play some video."

Vince groaned and finished his beer.

"We could go to the beach and smoke a joint."

"You got a joint, man? You've been holding a joint since I arrived and haven't fired it up? That's tyranny. Let's smoke it now," Vince ranted.

"Yeah right, so my neighbor Mr. State Patrol Bull could pop his head in and I'm busted all over again. Remember, he's got a nose like a bloodhound. He'd be over in seconds flat dressed up in his cop costume, cuffing my ass, taking me to prison."

"You got some kind of imagination, son."

"That's not imagination, cuz, that's paranoid mind in reflux." Tye looked out the window across the newly cut grass and the wet road at the State Patrol cruiser parked in the driveway. "I know he's listening to us right now. Bastard! I hope you heard that."

"Man, you are down for the count. Hey—yeah, yeah—I know what we can do, shit suree. I forgot all about this marvel of nature. We got entertainment at our doorstep and it's probably not raining. Torpedo told me last night."

"Torpedo's reliable. What's the scam, man?"

"They're going to blow up two whales on Dungeness Spit today."

"What?"

"Yeah, they're going to nuke some beluga. They washed up over on the spit and the clammers and shore dwellers are complaining because they stink so bad. So bingo, bango, whale guts city, baby." Vince did a little dead whale dance.

"That's not to be missed. Let's blow." Tye grabbed his jacket, headed for the kitchen, and opened the refrigerator

39

where he filled his pockets with cans of Rainier beer.

"Don't you got any Oly?" Vince looked over his shoulder into the refrigerator.

"No. My dad doesn't believe in that piss and either do I."

"Piss? And what is Rainier, the champagne of bottled beers?" Vince took a can of Rainier from the refrigerator. "Beggars can't be choosers." He shut the door behind him.

They both headed for the front door and grumbled as they ran to the truck, cussing the rain. They jumped in as a can of beer fell out of Tye's pocket. He scrambled, picking it up while keeping one eye on the house across the street, hoping he had not been seen.

"Did you see that? Shit sure, he saw it." Tye straightened himself still watching the house to see if anyone was looking.

"He didn't see anything, para-Freud. Relax, we're going to Sequim—dry land. The only thing it will be raining there is whale blubber." Vince revved the engine.

Tye laughed as Vince spun gravel and sped off. They spotted State Patrol Officer Clark watching them leave from his living room window. Tye waved. "See what I mean? He's always watching. I can't wait to get the hell out of this joint." Tye put his feet on the console and reached into the CD holder and took out the Eels CD. "This skip?" he asked.

"They all skip, thanks to tools like you who handle 'em like bricks." Vince took a left out of town on Highway 20 and they were on their way.

Tye pushed in the CD and listened to the Eels blast "Mr.

E's Beautiful Blues." "God damn right it's a beautiful day," Tye sang along.

"Torch that ska, man," Vince ordered as he drove out of Discovery Bay and merged onto Highway 101.

Tye dug into his coat pocket took out a beer and began the slow search for the joint, a search that turned into a panicked frisk. "Shit, where is it?" He patted his entire body.

"Don't tell me you lost it, man?" Vince sipped his beer watching the emerald green scenery swim by in sixty-mile-an-hour waves. Tye took his coat off to do a more thorough check on his coat and the CD player repeated the phrase, "I like birds," caught in the skip of the compact disc. They did not notice this as they both swore in different words about their dire straits due to the loss of the joint.

"Shit man, I wanted to be stoned to see whales blown to shit." Vince finished his beer and placed it under his seat. "How could you lose something like that," he complained, "and you're going to fucking college?" Vince stepped on the gas and the V8 purred to a higher gear, passing a slow-rolling tourist sucking in nature at a thirty-miles-an-hour snail's pace. "Tourists." Vince spat as he passed them.

Tye put Fat Boy Slim in the CD player and as he did Vince noticed it. Vince laughed so hard he went into convulsions trying hard to keep control of the car.

"What?" Tye asked dumbfounded.

"You dumb shit," Vince said as he reached over and plucked the joint out from behind Tye's ear.

Tye joined in the laughter and at the same time, as if

41

the gods separated the clouds, the sun shone like a burning zephyr and Tye and Vince laughed louder and waved good-bye to the rain that still fell behind them. They had entered Sequim, the desert of the Peninsula. Tye pushed in the lighter and waited for it to pop out. He opened his window as he lit the joint and sucked in the curtain of delicious smoke. He passed it to Vince without exhaling, held it, then blew it out in one steady slow blow.

They flew through Sequim Bay State Park and then through the town of Sequim and then headed north to the Dungeness River and the spit. Five miles out of town and the sun was gone and a gray pregnant sky warned of more rain.

"I wonder how much dynamite they're going to use?" Vince asked, sucking the last remains from the non-existent roach. He tossed it out the window and licked his burnt fingers.

"It looks like we're not the only one who heard about the whale explosion." Tye pointed ahead at parking that lined the road a good two miles from the beach. "Should we park here?"

"No, we'll get lucky." Vince gunned the Chevy and passed a slow filing of folks headed for the beach. At the parking lot a State Patrolman waved cars away.

"Oh no, shit!" Tye tried to duck and point. "It's him. How did he get here?"

"Jesus Christ, I don't know, but give me some gum and get that cologne in the glove compartment and spray."

Vince slowed down but had no choice but to drive right up to State Patrolman Clark. Tye passed him some gum nonchalantly and took some himself. He sprayed a blast of Stetson into the truck cabin ether. He rolled open his window.

"We cool," Vince sighed. Tye nodded his head. They pulled up along side Officer Clark.

"Hi, Mr. Clark," Tye greeted him, trying not to breathe.

"Tye, Vince. What are you boys doing here?" He wore mirrored sunglasses and Tye felt his eyes searching the cabin of the truck.

"I guess like everyone else, coming to watch some whales be blown up. We left before you, how did you beat us?" Tye asked, trying not to betray his highness that seemed to get higher.

"Short cuts. And as far as this event goes I gotta feeling these Park Rangers have no clue of what they're doing." Officer Clark looked toward the spit.

"That will even make it more worth watching," Vince said, smiling. "Any parking in the lot by any chance?" Vince seemed as cool as a cucumber to Tye.

"Nope, full up, but park over there in front of my cruiser and leave the keys in it."

"Wow, thanks, man," Vince hummed. "Our lucky day, Tye."

"Thanks, Mr. Clark," Tye said as Officer Clark waved them through. Tye closed the window and looked at amazement at Vince. "How high are you?"

"I'm looking down on high." Vince laughed, pulling in

behind the Highway Patrol cruiser.

"I hope you don't have any incriminating evidence in here. He'll search the place. Didn't you see him sniffing around?"

"No, all I saw was him being an outstanding citizen giving us a prime parking space," Vince said as he fingered through his ashtray looking for anything suspicious. "Nothing in here."

"What about the beer bottles under the seat?" Tye asked, zipping up his coat, readying himself for the sharp weather of the spit.

"I'll tell him they're my dad's," he said as he stepped out into the brisk damp weather.

"Yeah, right, like he might believe that." Tye slammed the door closed, feeling the beer cans in his large coat pockets.

"Hey, you can't argue with prime-time parking, my man." Vince squinted and led the way toward the crowd huddling on the spit.

"Yeah, that's a great defense in a court of law," Tye moaned, looking back at the truck and officer Clark suspiciously.

"Paranoia strikes deep, into parking it won't creep. Let's go watch some whale annihilation." Vince laughed. They walked out to Dungeness Spit, a huge sand bar at the mouth of the Puget Sound that stuck out like a big old tongue in the Strait of Juan de Fuca. It was said to be the biggest sand bar in the world. Whatever the size, it licked up its fair share of shit, everything from boats to whales.

Blowing up whales was a hard secret to keep in this part of the world. There were about three hundred people in small groups, smoking cigarettes, drinking beer, and waiting for the fireworks. There were clammers digging, some crazy kids skim-boarding, and a huddle of Park Rangers discussing their options. And then there was the smell, at first dulled by the fresh sea air and anomalies of the spit but then, with a whisk of a lost wind, they were faced with the gagging stench of rotting whale.

"God," Tye groaned, "I never smelled anything like that." They both stopped breathing through their noses.

Vince grimaced and pulled a beer from his coat, looking back to make sure he was out of sight of Officer Clark. "That is a stench from hell," Vince winced. "I hope they get this over with. I can't stand it. I'm going to puke."

Tye took a beer from his coat and they walked in the wet hard sand towards the various huddles, stopping at what was the outer edge of people, a thousand feet from the two carcasses. They were gray whales as big as small houses. People wrapped their mouths with scarves and held their sleeves over their noses to stop the wet offal of gag-inducing stench. They watched as three Park Rangers ran from the whales with a wire, one stopping to gag and then vomit. A group chuckle rose from the crowd.

They ran back to the group of Rangers who stood around the detonator about five hundred feet from the whales. "Looks likes it's going to happen." Vince drank more beer, his eyes watering from the stink.

"I wonder how much dynamite they planted?" Tye sipped his beer thought a stiff upper lip.

"Enough to blow up two fucking big whales," Vince chuckled, watching the Park Ranger wire the detonator. When it was done the group of eight Park Rangers looked back at the crowd in unison, readying the crowd for the whale explosion.

One Ranger lifted the detonator box dramatically and pushed the buttons. The explosion that ensued drew a huge "Wow!" from the crowd at the sight of the instant disintegration of the mammoth creatures. But before any other verbal reaction was possible, earth-shaking thuds of tons of whale meat, blubber and bones started to rain down. Three of the rangers were crushed under a one-ton chunk of whale. The crowd was sprayed with the stench. General panic ensued. Tye screamed at Vince who was already sprinting toward the parking lot. He was pelted with a piece of meat that hurled him face first into the sand. Vince stopped and helped him and they ran as fast as they could away. They saw Officer Clark with lights flashing, siren burning, driving on the spit toward the catastrophe. When he drove by he yelled out the window to get their truck and help. Vince and Tye looked back at the crowd. People were crying, weeping, sobbing, and screaming. It looked like a battlefield with dozens of people down and injured.

Vince and Tye looked at each other trying to make sense of it but they could not. They were covered with whale guts, blood and blubber. They ran to the truck and became an emergency ambulance driving two people to Sequim hospital who were suffering from head injuries. They left the hospital, dried whale gut still on them. They would remain in shock for days. They would tell the tale for years.

MISSING LINK

W hy did he play with the boy's mind so? It was like playing with dynamite. The boy was excitable and beating him in chess wasn't going to make him calm. He was a time bomb waiting to blow. I will have to try to calm him down with a little story, he thought.

He looked at his grandson, Lem Horn, staring mad into space, eighteen years old and anger enough for everyone. He didn't fit in his body. A gangly six foot three with little or no muscle and a belly that was not from drinking beer but from baby fat that hadn't left him. His eyes were set deep in his head, brown and shifting from intense to empty. He had just reached puberty and had grown four inches in the last year. He had been kicked out of school for fighting. He was being tutored so that he might get his GED certificate, not that it meant much. This was a kid who never had a chance from the get-up-and-go. He never had a father, just him and his less-than-motherly daughter. A cigarette dangled from the boy-man's mouth; a skint of smoke spiraled upward.

"Did you hear they found old Link Page dead up in the North Cascades?" he asked, trying to penetrate the silence.

"Nope," Lem answered, rage of the chess loss still filling him. How could I lose? he wondered to himself, knowing it was all about attention.

"You remember old Link Page don't you? Worked down at the mill. You met him over at our place a couple of times. You remember?"

"Sure." Lem held his anger and took a drag from his butt.

"You know he went and disappeared about five years ago, never seen again. Until now. Dead...." James Horn pushed his black horn-rim glasses back up his nose, making sure the boy was paying attention.

"So?" Lem grew impatient.

"You know why they called him Link, right?" James sat back, pressing back, adjusting in the easy chair, looking straight at the young man who sat across from him.

"No," Lem said. Distractions, that's what it was, he thought, not attention span, but the old man's distractions, still trying to justify the chess loss. And then like lightening in anger he backhanded the remaining chess players off the board, sending them on errant air travels to every corner of the shag-carpeted living room. It was a reaction without a thought and it made him feel better.

"What are you going to do, beat me up?" James Horn looked up at a now-grinning Lem. "Do you want to hear the story about Link or not?" he asked, defusing the bomb.

The boy was ugly. He sat back down slowly scratching the few whiskers that he called a beard, acne scars bright red with his agitation. His black hair was long and stringy and unwashed. He was a slob, orbiting worthlessness, waiting for something to happen and doing nothing to make it happen. The boy was dealing with a rebellious nature emanating from the core of his existence. His recent metamorphosis warped him even more. He had no clue about anything. He had no friends except for his left hand that he exercised regularly.

"Tell me about Link, already," Lem said impatiently, putting out his cigarette and lighting another one. Scars from cigarette burns spelled "Lem" on the back of his hand.

"He was blinding drunk down at the tavern, drinking Jack Daniels like it was water. He was babbling about leaving it all behind, heading into North Cascades and communing with nature. I never thought he would do it. When he didn't come back, I thought he drove to California or something. But he did do it. He goddamn did do it. Shit." James Horn shook his head in disbelief.

"So?" Lem interrupted. He himself had thought about leaving it all behind lately. He kicked the king across the room banging it against the wall.

"So? So, he did it! Some people think about it, some people talk about it, but I tell you no one ever does it. It just ain't natural. They found him supposedly hours after he died of a heart attack. That's what the autopsy said. The hikers said he had hair down to his waist. Beard, too. A regular Sasquatch." James Horn tried to visualize him.

"Are you trying to tell me he was Big Foot?" Lem sucked on his cigarette, raising his eyes into his head.

"No, he didn't have big feet, but funny thing is, his feet were the reason he got the nickname, Link," James Horn said and then laughed remembering something.

"Get on with it." Lem kicked a pawn this time; it tumbled across the brown shag carpet.

"What are you trying to do, lose the pieces?" his grandfather scolded him.

"It's my board. They're my players." Lem grabbed the last remaining player on the table, a knight, and stuck it in his mouth, sucked it in and pushed it out on his tongue.

"Do you think that's funny?" James Horn stood and began to gather the flung pieces.

"Yeah, a regular Seinfeld." Lem spat, put his feet on the table, and rocked his chair back, balancing the knight on his nose.

Watching this, James Horn purposely, but making it look as if it was an accident, kicked the chair leg, knocking Lem off balance, mak-ing him fall back. He fell in a heap. The thud was painful to listen to. Lem was up in a flash of anger and in his grandfather's face, ready to fight. "What are you doing, old man!" he screamed.

"Picking up after you," James Horn said, not flinching, analyzing the gawky boy's anima.

"You did that on purpose," Lem accused his grandfather.

"On purpose? Why would I do that?" James Horn picked up the king and placed it on the chessboard and began to arrange the board again, sipping on his spiked coffee.

"Even my grandfather has a vendetta," Lem whimpered, sitting back down, lighting another cigarette.

"Vendetta?"

"You heard me," Lem said.

"I heard you but I don't believe you. Why would I have a vendetta against you? Why would anybody have a vendetta against you? I think you been smoking too much of that wacky tobaccy." James Horn continued setting up the board. "I mean who on earth would have a vendetta against you and why?"

Lem thought about the vendetta business, about how this had become a theme in his life, how it was real. It was a nightmare he dealt with constantly. He could not do anything and the more effort he would put into it, the harder was the resistance, until there was nothing left but anger. "Life!" he yelled, accusing it of having the vendetta.

"Lem, you have delusions. You're not important enough for life to be out to get you," James Horn teased.

"Thanks." Lem sat back down, thinking about his unimportance, pissed off, sulking, but still thinking that his grandfather did not know, had not witnessed the power of that force that did not want him to succeed at anything.

"I'm kidding." James Horn noticed a flinch of hurt cross his grandson's brow.

53

"Sure," Lem groaned, hopeless. "Maybe I should kill my-self. Better yet, head out into the wilderness and become a Sasquatch like your friend, Link...." He took a deep drag of the Salem and blew it out toward the cigarette stained ceiling.

James Horn looked at the boy, starting to feel bad for making him feel bad. He straightened the board and ad-justed the players. Finally, he took one black pawn and one white pawn, put them behind his back, switched the pawns between his hands then stuck his fisted hands in front of Lem to choose one.

"I'm not playing." Lem looked away from his grand-fa-ther's fists.

James Horn did not drop his fists. He couldn't help teas-ing the boy.

"Get your fucking fists out of my face!" Lem yelled and with a ferocious lunge and sweeping backhand sent the chessboard and pieces flying, again. "Don't you fucking understand me!"

"I guess you said you're not playing." James Horn chuck-led. He sat back, still holding onto the pawns, staring at the destruction. It was his fault; he knew it would happen but he could not help doing it. What else can you do when you're old? It's too late to leave it all behind as Link did. Too late for a lot of things. You have to get your entertainment when you can, he thought, trying to justify the tormenting of his grandson. "So what do you want to do?" James Horn asked, looking at the tortured boy.

"Go into the wilderness!" Lem screamed, his face pulsating red.

"Well then go," James Horn dared him, "but remember, there's no Twinkies out there or Ho-Ho's, no TV, no computers, no nothing, no smokes."

"I don't need nothing!" the boy barked, spitting his cigarette out.

James Horn recognized a ring of familiarity in Lem's tone and thought again of Link Page. He said he was going to do it, and he did. But then again, he was a grown man, lost in this life, confused and bewildered by life's procession to death. The only thing he could do was escape to the wilderness. He looked at the boy suspiciously. One year out of high school and he hadn't done anything, except grow. What had made him so angry? The idea of growing up, the responsibility? He was a genius as a child, at least that's what the tests said, learned how to play chess at six and beat him soundly then. A genius of ineptness. Now he can't even beat an old man, James Horn thought sadly.

"So how did Link get his name?" Lem asked angrily. He didn't want to be here anymore.

"Oh yeah, that." James Horn sipped his coffee. "We were swimming once out at the quarry. Link was a really good swimmer. Then I noticed something wrong with his feet and I pointed it out to him. He was embarrassed but showed me his four toes on each foot had webs between them. He had webbed feet! It was the strangest thing I'd ever seen. They looked like frog's feet. I started calling him 'the missing link,' and we charged kids a dime to look at his feet. A dime in those days was a lot of money. Link and I split the profit," James Horn reminisced.

"And he kept the name?" Lem scoffed.

"Yes, he did; in fact he liked the name. I think he liked it because it made him different. He liked being different, having something nobody else did." Thoughts of his childhood made James Horn get goose flesh.

"So why did he go to the wilderness if he was so fucking special?" Lem asked.

"I don't know. That last night I was with him it was all just drunken talk, nothing I could understand. He had been on the bottle a long time. In fact he was always on the bottle. I was mostly off the bottle but when it happened I was on. What I think it was, was that at forty, no wife, working down at the mill for twenty years, getting drunk every night, he came to realize how unimportant he was, even with webbed feet. He could not live with that. So he found refuge in the solitude of the wilderness," James Horn eulogized. "Nobody ever dreamed he would stay out there for ten years though. Hell, nobody knew he was out there. I don't think Link would have expressed it exactly like that, but that's what I think."

"What makes you the expert?" Lem asked.

"I'm not an expert. It's my opinion." James Horn turned back to the boy.

"What good is your opinion?"

"Good as the next guy's." James Horn sat back and threw one of the pawns at Lem who caught it. Holding the piece reminded him of the chess game again, about his loss. He threw it at the wall hard and yelled at his grandfather, "You don't know anything! You don't think that I'll go into the wilderness! You don't think I will, do you?" Lem's eyes were as big walnuts.

"You don't have any reason." He returned Lem's hot look.

"Is that what you think?" Lem paced, ranting. "You don't think I have a reason to get the hell out of here? To leave this crap life behind? You're an old man who knows nothing."

"You're a young man who hasn't gotten off his fat ass and done anything." His eyes flashed at the boy.

"What do you know? You're from the generation that has made this shit world we now live in." His jaw was set. "Your way to fix what's wrong is to learn how to work a computer. That will make life easy."

"You have such a hard life! Look around! Stop your whining and be a man!" James Horn lost his temper.

"What does a man do? Go to the wilderness, like your friend? I'll go to the goddamn wilderness!" Lem yelled. "That's easy!"

"Then be gone! Leave me and take your dramatics. If you're going to the wilderness, go! It's quite a drive to get there, three hours to Ross Dam. That'd be your best entry point. You better get a move on; it'll be dark soon. But what is darkness to someone who will live the rest of his life out there?" He pointed to nowhere.

Lem's face flushed red with the furor of being dared. He stormed to the door, looked back at his rocking grandfather and yelled: "I'm gone!" He slammed the door so hard that pictures shook on the walls.

James Horn sat listening to the revving of Lem's truck, then to the screeching of his tires up the street, the last exclamation point of his anger. He stood up and began picking up the chess pieces, wondering about this bluff, thinking about Link that drunken night. He didn't believe Link would go, but he did….

James Horn looked out the picture window at the quiet rural street, then out over the timberline at the Cascades ominously rising around the looming snow-covered Mount Rainier. A feeling suddenly anguished him, but it was too late to stop the boy.

FALLING FROM THE SKY

Tug tossed the paper airplane at the blank TV screen. The rain pounded the cheap single-pane window. How long could he drive around in a circle in the rain? He had been driving a loop around the Puget Sound for two weeks and it hadn't stopped raining the entire time. And more than just rain had been falling from the sky. He had completed the loop ten times.

The loop started in Tacoma via Highway 16 to Port Gamble, a ferry ride to Highway 104, on to Highway 101, another ferry ride to Whidbey Island, to Highway 20, then to Burlington where he would take I-5 south to Everett through Seattle and back to Tacoma. The drive had become a melange of cheap hotels, bad bars, and fast food. Now he was in Everett again, contemplating it all. First cows, then UFO's—they took his mind off what he intended to do. A sardonic whistle came to his lips but disappeared when it could find no direction, no tune to blow. Tug sat up on the hard bed letting his mind churn until he grew restless thinking, Would this be the time? He rolled over on his stomach and masturbated.

Red neon and more red neon spilt into the room from the sign that blinked The Sleeper Hotel, lighting the road the parking lot, and the relentless rain. This was the third time he had stayed here. Tug had asked for a room away from the light but there was no escaping it.

Tug walked out of the bathroom through the main room, zipping up his pants, out the door into the red neon night barefoot in the rain. There were three pick-ups and a station wagon in the lot. He opened the door at the office. Bells rang and he looked up at the surveillance camera that watched. He heard a TV blaring behind the partition that separated the front from the back. A very fat woman with a grimace of someone suffering from hemorrhoids appeared from behind the partition.

"What can I do?"

"You got any beer?" He knew they did because he had bought beer there before. Tug noticed the cleavage of the woman. Her tits were huge. He looked at her gnarled face. She pointed at a refrigerator that stood in the corner of the room. The room was a coffee table with a couple of beaten magazines pell mell on it and an end table with a lamp that lit the dinginess but couldn't usurp the ever-prevalent red neon. Tug opened the refrigerator door and leaned on it, balancing, looking at his choice, Miller Lite or Oly.

"This it?" Tug asked, looking back at her, remembering he had bought Corona here the last time. She nodded. Tug leaned back into the refrigerator and pulled out a six-pack of Oly. "How much?"

"Ten dollars."

"Ten dollars?" Tug groaned.

"Yup," she deadpanned.

"That's robbery."

"No, that's the price. Closest store is the 7-11 if you want to go. She waited for the money. Tug fished a crumbled ten-dollar bill from his wallet and handed it to her and walked out not saying anything more. Red neon, relentless rain.

He shot-gunned the first two beers trying to get rid of the buzz in his head. He thought about them again. All he wanted to do was forget, but he couldn't. That's why he had to do what he had to do. No one knew him anymore. After each beer Tug would crush the can by placing it between his hands and, pushing it like a squeezebox, would flatten it. And then he would throw the can out his opened door and hear it skid across the asphalt. After five beers he took his boots off, closed the door, and cried sorrowfully. How could you explain something like this? What had he done to deserve this? His wife was pregnant by his best friend. He began to cry again and fell asleep.

He woke scared and sweating, dreaming that he was being examined by aliens. He was sure he felt an anal probe. He shook his head, not believing that he was actually contemplating believing in UFO's and aliens. A month ago he would have choked on his beer in laughter at someone who claimed to believe. But he had seen them on Whidbey

Island lined up like a diamond, changing direction on a dime, starting and stopping in the blink of an eye. Zero to ten thousand miles per hour in about two seconds.

But even that could not stop him contemplating murdering them.

He opened the last beer and obsessed about what he could do, his mind running in circles just like the trip. His twenty-gauge shotgun was under his seat ready and waiting. Every time he drove through Tacoma, he drove closer and closer to his house thinking he might do it. Blow their mother-fucking heads off. He imagined finding them in bed and just unloading both barrels. It actually gave him some relief from the constant throbbing of his head. He finished the beer while he dressed and headed out the door of the motel with exactly what he had come with, nothing. He jumped in his truck and spun the wheels on the wet pavement. The morning was dull and gray with sprinkles. The red neon, now, nothing but a thread of pulsating light.

He needed gas so he headed for a Quick Stop he saw just before the exit to I-5. He would drive back toward Tacoma again. They had been married for five years; the last three had been all grief from their inability to have a child. The doctor said his sperm count was low but high enough to still conceive, but it seemed as if it would never happen. He ended up having an affair in a drunken guilt-laden venture that she found out about. He thought they had patched things up, but a year later there was good old Stan, his best friend, the other drywall expert at Simpson's construction, fucking his wife at lunch when he was supposedly visiting his sick mother at the hospital. Stan the man needed to die.

He would have already done it if not for the things falling from the sky. Besides the UFO sighting, he had seen something else that was way beyond his comprehension. It was on Whidbey Island again; he was drunk, driving at night, trying to get to Oak Harbor and another cheap hotel when he had to take a pee, so he pulled over and walked into a large field where he unzipped his pants and let rip a long-held urination that tore through his urethra, forcing a sigh that seemed to even make the rain halt for a second. As he zipped back up, he heard an enormous thud and, looking up, he saw two cows fall from the sky and bounce with thundering thuds in the field. He was awe-struck, rubbing his eyes and pinching himself, swearing off alcohol for life. So shocked was he by the hallucination, he did not want to investigate. When he did finally get the nerve to take a closer look, he walked to where he imagined the cows landed. There the carcasses lay and, when he examined them closer, he discovered they were cows all right, completely disemboweled. He looked up at the sky in disbelief and then ran back to the truck as if he had done something illegal. He burned rubber out of there and never looked back.

He pulled into the Quick Stop and filled his truck up with gasoline. At over a buck fifty a gallon, his circular tour was getting expensive. He had plenty of money, though. He had been working steady for ten years and saved religiously. He paid the Filipino cashier for a six-pack of Corona and some beef jerky. When he stepped out of the store he noticed a tall white-haired kid looking at his truck.

"Can I help you?" he asked the boy with a bit of an edge.

"No, just looking at the cherry truck, man. Slashin'." the boy looked up, soaked to the skin, touching the customized paint job. He was very tall, acne-scarred, and wore dark glasses in a rainstorm. His whiteness made his over-sized coat not noticeable.

Tug stared at him, curious but appreciating the boy's compliments. His '56 Chevy truck was his pride and joy.

"It's flawless. How does it cook?" the ghost-colored boy asked.

"It cooks," Tug said, opening the door and throwing the bag of beer and jerky into the cabin. He took his shotgun from under the seat and placed it in the gun rack across the window, feeling the boy's eyes on him. When he looked up after closing the door, the boy was standing by the passenger door, knocking on the window. Tug rolled it down. "Yeah?"

"I was wondering if you were going south if you could give me a ride?"

"Nope." Tug rolled the window back up and backed the truck out. He did not leave, though; something stopped him. It was something sorrowful within himself. Maybe after driving around by himself for so long, he needed someone to talk to. He stopped the truck, beeped the horn and waved the boy over. "Get in," he said, not quite sure if this was the greatest idea.

"Thanks man, thanks. I'm going to Olympia." The boy lumbered into the passenger's side. He was gangly, well over six foot tall. He barely fit in the seat. "My name's Whitey."

"Whitey?" Tug chuckled.

"For obvious reasons," Whitey said, settling himself in the seat.

"Mine's Tug, and I'll get you as far as Tacoma," he said, and he headed for the I-5 south entrance. He looked at the boy out of the corner of his eye. The acne wasn't as bad as it first seemed. His skin was so white that the slightest irritation was an inflamed red. He wore black horn-rims that were tinted purple and his hair was long and scraggly, hanging below a soaked sock hat that had a Mariners emblem on it. Where his skin was not irritated you could see his bulging green veins. His hands are what struck Tug. They were huge, as big as a foot. He had them on his thighs and they reached from knee to waist. He leaned forward watching the road. An odd creature, Tug thought.

"What are you going to Olympia for?" Tug asked, still not believing those hands.

"Back to school," Whitey said, as he tore Velcro straps apart on his coat and pulled out an Apple powerbook computer in its case from under it.

Tug watched him place the computer on his lap. "Where do you go to school?" he asked, wondering why he was carrying a computer around in a rainstorm.

"Evergreen," Whitey said, without taking his eyes off the rain soaked four-lane highway in front of them.

65

"Oh," Tug answered, knowing the reputation of the free-wheeling, cavorting, open college. "Do you like it?"

"It's all right."

"What do you study?"

"Computer programming," Whitey said, tapping his computer and letting out a half laugh. "You know, one of those computer geeks. Never goes anywhere without it."

Tug nodded.

"This is one of the computers that make up my life. Is that your gun?" Whitey looked back at the polished and shined shotgun, touching the metal.

"Yeah," Tug replied.

"Kill anybody lately?" Whitey snickered.

Tug did not say anything, watching the rain pound the windshield and the windshield wipers try in vain to disperse it. Suddenly he was imagining the scene of him breaking into the bedroom, shotgun in hand, catching them in bed together and blowing their brains away. It gave him a rush of adrenaline and he reached down into his paper bag and pulled out a beer and twisted the top off while steering with his knees. He almost forgot Whitey was there, his fantasy was so vivid.

"You know I was just kidding about killing?" Whitey blinked. "Can I have a beer?"

"You old enough? I wouldn't want to be contributing to the delinquency of a minor," Tug said as he lifted a Corona from the bag and handed it to Whitey without letting him answer.

Whitey's hand engulfed the bottle. He twisted the top and took a long drink. "So what do you shoot with it?" he asked.

Tug looked at Whitey with a smile, picturing their faces. "Birds," he said.

Whitey took another drink. He wiped his brow mockingly. "Whew. For a minute I thought you were going to say hitchhikers."

Tug raised his eyebrows and smiled. "So what do you think, I-5 or 405?"

"I-5 express lanes, bro; it's the only way to go," Whitey said, still trying to get comfortable.

Tug nodded, having done this ten times and counting, he preferred the trip through Seattle on I-5 to Tacoma rather than the S-curved 405 circumnavigating the city. He liked the Seattle skyline, seeing it rise up from Elliott Bay, even though in the rain it was just a gray rainy mirage from the highway.

"You live in Tacoma?" Whitey tapped his thumb on top of the bottle.

Tug did not answer, not knowing. Where did he live now? He could never call that place his home again. The only thing he could call home was his truck. "Nope," he answered.

"Work there?"

"Not anymore." Tug grimaced.

Whitey took another drink and took a deep breath, watching Northgate Mall fly by and noticing the express lanes were closed. "Too bad," he sighed.

Tug shrugged his shoulders and finished his beer speeding past two cars like they were standing still. The rain drenched the windshield putting the wipers to the test. They weren't the original wipers but a pair he had to customize a bit to work on the '56 Chevy.

"Fucking rain, man," Whitey whined, "it's worse than finding a friend fucking your wife." The words fell out of Whitey's mouth as an often-told refrain but Tug did not like the suggestion or the improbable realm of coincidence.

"What?" Tug felt himself trembling suddenly and his grip tightened on the steering wheel.

"Just joking around." Whitey felt the tension.

"No, what did you say?" Tug took his eyes off the road and stared a bullet at Whitey.

"Relax man, I said nothing." Whitey sucked his beer, watching the road.

"No, you said something about your wife sleeping with your best friend."

"I don't have a wife, and I really don't have a best friend. I was just describing how bad this rain is. It's been raining for years. It's driving people crazy. Makes them see and hear things that aren't really there."

Tug watched Whitey say the words, biting his lower lip unconsciously. An anger rose in Tug and like a flash he grabbed for Whitey's throat, swerving on the wet highway; but as if by magic, Whitey simultaneously grabbed Tug's hand in a vice grip and straightened the steering wheel so the truck came back to equilibrium. Tug felt the magnified squeeze of Whitey's grip until he finally screamed out in pain and Whitey released his hand.

"What's wrong with you? I didn't mean anything by it." Whitey stared in disbelief at Tug. There was silence as they slid by the University of Washington and saw the first sky scrapers of Seattle's skyline rise through the gray. The rain receded and all that was left was the sound of driving and thinking about what had just happened.

"Sorry," Tug finally apologized, knowing something had to be said, an explanation to end the silence. "Well, for one thing, you're right about this rain. I have been seeing some weird things."

"Like what?" Whitey asked curiously.

"Like UFO's and cows falling from the sky," Tug said sheepishly, and he grabbed into the bag for another beer.

"UFO's? Cow's dropping from the sky? Where?" Whitey asked, not even flinching at the absurdity.

"Whidbey Island," Tug answered, finding Whitey's continence disconcerting.

"Yeah, that makes sense," Whitey said knowingly.

"What makes sense? UFO's and cows falling from the sky do not make sense." Tug shook his head and watched the Space Needle float in and out of the clouds.

"It makes sense it would be there. It could be anywhere, but there you have Whidbey Naval Air Station and a high level of military testing."

"You're saying what I saw was created by the US government?" Tug laughed, then straightened himself up. "Okay,

I can go along with the UFO's being some kind of military secret, but cows falling from the skies? Explain that one to me." He drank from his beer and saluted the Rainier Brewery as they drove by.

"Well, from what I've read and heard, it's the old Beam-Me-Up-Scotty Project," Whitey said, sticking his thumb in his bottle to make a deep bass-like twang.

"Beam-Me-Up-Scotty Project?" Tug almost spat his beer up in laughter.

"Yeah, it seems the government has been testing some molecular transporting, but in the process they're disemboweling a lot of cows. It's all right with me. The sooner they perfect it the faster we can all be transporting all around the world. And instead of dicking around in this rain we could be beamed to Hawaii or something." Whitey drank the remainder of his beer. "But you didn't attack me because you saw UFO's or saw cows falling from the sky. Why did you attack me?" He scratched his neck where Tug had tried to strangle him.

Tug looked at Whitey, not believing what he just heard but realizing that it was as good of a reason as he could come up with, and he suddenly wished he could be beamed up, too. That's when he broke down and began to tell his story. "Yeah, you're right. The reason I attacked you had nothing to do with that. It had to do with what you said. You see, my wife did sleep with my best friend, not only slept with and fucked him but also got goddamned pregnant by him."

Tug confessed all as they flew through the many shades of gray rain in the Renton valley, past Sea-Tac International Airport up the crescent to the Puyallup Valley and into Tacoma. Before he had ended his pitched story, his anger and pain boiling up again and again, he realized that he had driven to his street and he was in front of his house. He parked across the street from it, staring at the empty driveway, wondering if they were in there. Whitey sat next to him, silent, staring, too.

"What are you going to do?" Whitey finally asked, sticking his finger in his beer bottle again.

Tug looked at him and then the gun and then the house.

"You could go in and blow their brains out. They certainly deserve it. Shit, I feel like going in there and killing the evil, fucking scum. They are all that is wrong with the world. But then again, this silly society that we live in doesn't take much to murderers, especially murderers who kill pregnant women, no matter how they got pregnant. But I guess when you pull that trigger, you kill not only them but all the hurt, pain, and horror you've been carrying around. Who wouldn't want to kill that, expunge it, and annihilate it? I would."

Tug looked at Whitey letting his words echo in his silent rage.

"Of course, after you do it, their pain is over, but yours has just begun, unless you decide to take your own life, too. Then all is solved and everything goes to black in your corner of the world. But of course you could give some pain and get some relief and have a few laughs while you do it. You could make their lives living hell."

Tug had never been closer to doing the deed, but the last statement Whitey made confused him. He shook his head, not getting it. "What's worse than dying?"

Whitey chuckled tapping the computer on his lap, "Well a little unexpected credit card debt for one."

"What?" The suggestion shattered Tug's fixation with murder.

"Not to mention an IRS audit, a phone bill that grows exponentially, a default on a loan, and perhaps even a criminal record." Whitey smirked.

"What?" Tug repeated, dumbfounded. "What are you talking about?"

"Those are just a few of the things I am capable of unleashing on those poor excuses for human beings with this little machine right here." Whitey lifted the laptop and smiled.

It slowly sunk in and Tug started to smile as he thought about it. "Can you really do those things?" he asked, suspiciously.

"Can the government make cows fall from the sky?" Whitey laughed. "I can do that and a lot more faster than you can say Bill Gates. All I need is a phone jack and some information that only a best friend—or a husband—might have." Whitey winked.

Tug shook his head as he felt a great burden lifted. Coincidentally or not, the sun exploded though the gray shroud and bounced off the shine of his truck. He started to laugh and then just kept repeating one word: "Yeah, yeah, yeah, yeah. Let's go find you a phone jack." He started the truck and revved the motor and spun the tires on the wet asphalt, feeling the sweet taste of revenge and the giddiness of payback. Whitey smiled and the sunshine broke through the clouds falling from the sky in sheets of light.

A STORY NOT TO BE BELIEVED

I t was a wringing wet morning. Fog and rain playing games with shades of gray. He could barely
see in front of the El Camino. Moist soup. The windshield
wipers dragged the wet away from the window and his line
of vision. He bent over the steering wheel peering through
a small clear hole in the saturate. He didn't have to see to
drive this stretch of Highway 20 on Whidbey Island. He
knew it well, every bump, every turn, every place a state or
county bull would consider putting on the radar. He knew
how many guardrail posts there were on the road from his
house to his job at the state game farm ten miles away. He
had counted them on too many occasions to get a consen-
sus. One thousand nine hundred and fifty-six guardrail
posts from home to the farm.

The rain would stop and the fog would burn off by noon.
He would be done with the watering by then and on his
way home. He would be out water-skiing by two o'clock on

Campbell Lake enjoying the August sun. That was the plan. The cassette played but he didn't listen. The fog filled his mind and the rhythm of the windshield wipers made him drift into a smooth slalom run on the lake.

'This fog better burn off,' he thought. For the last week it had been staying foggy until late morning; then the sun full of heat would warm enough to melt it away. It would start with patches of blues, turn to drifting cumulus clouds and then be crystal clear by noon. It was a ritual the ocean, land, and sky went through. An ancient ritual that had been repeated on Whidbey Island since the power of glaciers and the art of nature formed the elongated island that lies like a vein of emerald in the mouth of Puget Sound.

He cracked his window to see if he could smell the tide in Penn's Cove. A raw smell seeped in and he immediately knew where he was, San de Fuca, the no-town-at-all, that lay midway on his journey to work. He liked the smell here where the road ran so close to the water at high tide that waves would sometimes splash onto the asphalt. It was a cove that still held its history; the smell of oysters, mussels, and clams; the home of countless Indian potlatches. And on the hill overlooking the cove was the gnarly old oak they called the hanging tree because it was used to that purpose back in the old days.

On occasions killer whales ventured into the cove to rest and gulp up some silver salmon when they ran, not to mention spawning smelt that made the grainy sand glow at night. It was the perfect halfway point either on his way to work or the way home. He had been working at the State Game Farm for four summers since his junior year in high school. It was good money, 'state wage,' outdoor work, the perfect way to pass the summers before going back to school. He gunned the engine of his El Camino up the shallow grade toward Coupeville. He was now only ten minutes away.

He worked alone on Saturdays. They were half days and all that was necessary was to water the fields. It was an easy job. With brush in hand you would walk the runs and fields where pheasants at various stages in their development would be hatched, would grow, and would finally be released into the wild for hunters to kill. Throughout the vast farm there was a watering system that used floats that hovered in a large metal pan. The float added water when the level went below a certain point. The watering process involved emptying the pan of old water, scrubbing as you did, and then centering the empty pan under the float where it would be filled automatically to the proper level. This was done on a daily basis so that disease would not be transmitted through the water.

It was ironic that the purpose of the farm and his job was to keep these Chinese ringneck pheasants healthy and alive so that they could be released, hunted, and killed. Keeping pheasants alive wasn't as easy as it might seem. Besides disease, there were pilings, rats, and dogs, not to mention hawks and owls.

And as of late these winged predators had been staging a slaughter of huge proportions in the outer fields feasting on brailed pheasant that were unable to hide or fly away. The rash of killings lately had convinced Wayne, the superintendent of the farm, to put up pole traps.

It was the rule of the Washington State Game Department that a balanced nature was at stake when a population of twenty thousand brailed birds ran around defenseless and were advantageously killed by predators. To solve the problem, someone had to kill these predators in order to settle the eco-system or balance nature.

The pole traps were made from an eight-foot post with a strong wire running the length of it. The wire was attached to the side of the post at both ends by fencing staples. This wire served as the guide wire for the varmint trap. A chain attached to the trap was threaded to the guide wire at the last link so when the trap was tripped it could fall freely to the ground. The varmint trap was set by pulling back its jaws and placing the trigger bar under the perch, a small metal disk in the middle of the jaws. In all the trap was six inches across when open. The set trap would be placed delicately on top of the pole where three nails had been hammered forming points of a triangle that fit around the perch and held the trap in place. The pole trap would be tied with wire alongside a fence post so that it stood three feet above the fence. This would create a perch where the owls and hawks would light and size their prey—brailed, defenseless pheasants. But when they landed on a pole trap they would be caught, try to fly, and then fall helplessly to the ground along the guide wire. The trap biting the talons would not kill the predator but leave it thrashing its wings trying to fly away but stopped by the chain. Then the captured bird would be either released or killed by the unlucky worker who would find it.

Dealing with a trapped, very angry bird was not easy. He still didn't have the knack or the stomach for it. He had only dealt with two incidents this season. One, a red-tail hawk that he had released since the trap had not maimed the talon. Releasing was more difficult than killing. Killing was a relatively simple job of getting the attention of the captured bird and then unleashing a blow to the head with the heavy scrub brush used to clean the watering pans. Releasing was a patient, scary dance of distraction and quickness. Either way was serious business.

It had stopped raining but the fog held on tight as he watched guardrail post number 800 go by barely visible. He tried to forget about hawks and owls. It was a needless worry anyway; hawks and owls would not be hunting in the fog. He veered left off Highway 20 up the gravel-strewn access road that led to the parking lot of the game farm. He gunned his engine before he entered the driveway and small pebbles were scattered like feed. He pulled into his regular parking place in front of storage barn. He turned off the ignition, shifted it into neutral, and glided to a stop. He sat staring out at the gray.

He finally stepped out of the car figuring the sooner he was done the sooner he would be water-skiing. He looked at the tractor and feed trailer that peeked out of the granary, then he turned and walked toward the incubator room that was attached to the main office. Past the main office and directly across from the granary was the main barn where the state game trucks were parked. Three other buildings made up the rest of the compound: Wayne's house stood at the road; the assistant superintendent's house, Ray's, was set back beside the granary; the main garage and public bathrooms stood in the middle of the gravel lot. All of these buildings were surrounded by islands, peninsulas, and isthmuses of well-manicured lawns, greener than green. Keeping the grounds was one of his jobs; immaculate was the rule; not even a cigarette butt could be found in the gravel. This was a state operation and therefore represented the state of Washington, the Evergreen, Ever-clean State. It was his job to keep the Game Farm as such. This fanatical anality didn't bother him; in fact, since starting to work there, he had begun to appreciate order.

He opened the door to the incubator room, stepped inside and pulled the chain light on. He looked at the wall of egg-turning bins and then at the sink. Alongside the sink was a towel bar where the brushes hung. The brushes were wooden and substantial, weighing about a pound with stiff inch-long bristles. He took a brush, pulled the light chain off, walked outside, and closed the door behind him. The fog engulfed the whole farm. The wooden brush felt good in his hand and he spun it effortlessly having become intimate with this tool of the trade. His knee-high rubber boots dragged the wet gravel.

To water was an easy job, a simple action. A swirl of the brush around the metal water pans to loosen the algae that had collected over night, the emptying of the pan, another swirl of the brush to the dry pan, and then the placing of the pan back in its position below the float-gauged faucet. The water would rush down, filling the pan, and would turn off when the float came to the full level. A simple task that would have to be performed hundreds of times.

He began with the brooder houses that strung out like tentacles from the main complex. There were seventy-five brooder houses, lined up in tens, with five more circling the main barn. Brooder houses were small, eight feet by eight feet, where pheasant chicks lived out the first months of their lives. When they were old enough a small sliding door was opened so they could wander outside to a narrow enclosed runway. After this stage they were herded to a larger enclosed wired pen, and from there they were brailed so they could not fly and placed in the large fields that made up three quarters of the Game Farm. Every house, pen, and field had Chinese ring-neck pheasants in them now, and every one of these had to be watered. It was a three-hour job without any hitches.

He opened the wire gate to the first brooder house. He would start with these, move on to the wired pens, and then lastly walk the long treks up the field's fences where the pole traps were. He walked down the run that was worn from the trampling of pheasants. A couple of curious pheasants pulled their heads out from under their wings and looked dumbly at him. He came to his first pan, ducked down, tipped the pan slightly, circled the brush twice, poured the rest of the water over the wired stand that the pan sat on, and slid the pan back under the faucet centering the float, then stood up, the mundaneness begun.

He moved on to the larger covered pens. These pheasants were larger but not yet colored. A mature Chinese ring-neck pheasant was richly colored in reds, browns, and yellows and had a black ring of feathers around its neck that was highlighted by white down that trimmed the ring. They were a beautiful bird, but dumb. Their dumbness was witnessed by the fact that if he made any motion out of the ordinary, they would try to fly away, battering the wire that was strung above them and causing a cascade of water to fall on his head. Today he had not worn a hat, and that made him as dumb as the bird. But instead of returning to the main office to get a hat, he trudged on, bearing up to the scattered showers unleashed from the catacombed chicken wire. He was soaked when he finished the brooder runs and walked out into the open fields.

The pheasants that were in the fields were fully colored. The green leather brail that prevented them from flying was a bright contrast to the brown and red wing feathers. The brail was a y-shaped leather strap that was placed around the wing, over the flight feather, and pinned with a clip. It was simple yet effective. When the pheasants tried to fly, they would awkwardly flop and fall like a tossed rubber chicken. There were twelve fields all about seven hundred and fifty feet long and three hundred feet wide. There were two water pans per side. He moved past hoppers that held the feed. They were long aluminum house-shaped bins. The roofs came off so that grain could be put in. On a regular day he would be checking these to see if they needed to be filled, but today he ignored them, having fed the day before.

Out in the fields the fog was so heavy he could not see from one end of a field to the other. His rubber boots glistened with moisture. The wooden brush was a part of his hand now and he twirled it unconsciously. Occasionally, when he was approaching a water pan, maybe ten yards from it, he would throw the brush trying to hit the float. Seven times out of ten he would hit the pan. He looked up to see if the pole traps were in sight. They were in the last field he would have to water. That was four fields away. He could not see them yet, still holding onto the idea that owls and hawks would not hunt in fog.

He moved on like a bullet as wet as the day. The last field stood partly invisible in front of him. The invisible part shrouded in fog was where the pole traps were. And then he heard it, the clank of the chain against the lead wire. There was a trapped bird waiting for him. His pace slowed a bit.

The barn owl sat beside the pole staring at him with yellow eyes. It hissed and tried to fly away. Its eyes were ferocious, yellow beams of fear. It clicked its beak loudly, pulled back its head and hissed. It spread its wings and charged pulling up short when the trap moved no farther. It repeated this charge time after time, pulling at the guide wire recklessly. The wingspan was near six feet. The owl's trapped frenzy was powerful and scary. All he could do was watch the owl and feel his own heart pound with fear, wondering what he was going to do?

He decided not to kill the owl. The talon was intact. He walked toward the owl, praying, trying to remember the tricks of releasing. The owl lunged at him as he closed in, and then retreated, spreading its wings to their fullness. It hissed; it stood ready, viciously, for any error he might make. He tried to be brave, but he felt his hands trembling and the brush was like rubber in his hand. He wanted to move quickly but couldn't, hypnotized by the wildness of the owl. He stepped forward and waved his brush taking the owl's attention, and from the back he stepped on the owl's head, gently pinning it to the ground. But before he could pin the owl's free talon down, it was cutting through his wet rubber boot, sinking into his foot.

Without thinking he swung a roundhouse with his brush at the owl's head but missed. The owl pulled itself to his leg and covered it with feathers pecking at him with rabid energy. He swung the brush at the owl again and grazed its shoulder. The owl held on and tripped him sending him to his back, defenseless. He screamed and kicked, pulling at the pole, tearing it away from the fence post. The pole fell and on impact the staple that held the guide wire to the pole pulled loose. He kicked blindly as the owl pecked at him. Sweat poured down his face, feathers flew. He finally unleashed a blow with the brush that stunned the owl, forcing it to let go its death grip. The owl backed away, the trap still wrapped around its talon but no longer connected to the pole guide wire. Realizing its partial freedom, it tried to fly but failed and then tried again and clumsily flapped its wings and rose up into the fog the trap still attached to its talon.

He pulled his foot and leg to his face, tore off his boot and rolled up his pant leg. There was no blood, but a bruise was quickly appearing on his shin. He put his boot back on, rolled down his pant leg, and walked quickly and with a slight limp back to the barn. He did not finish watering the last field and, walking back, he could not believe what had just happened. He stopped several times to gather himself and stop his trembling.

He wanted to tell someone but nobody was there. He locked up the office and sat in his El Camino, still in a hazy state of shock, massaging his leg. 'That owl had a vendetta,' he thought to himself, and he laughed, happy that he could laugh about it. He pulled out of the driveway, spinning gravel, and headed home, eleven o'clock and the fog still shrouding the highway. He did not take his eyes off the road, played no radio, and kept replaying the owl attack in his mind. He shook his head and talked to himself sternly: "You're all right; nothing happened; get over it. You're not owl food." He popped in Rage Against the Machine on his cassette deck and played it as loud as it could go, trying to

85

put an exclamation mark on his resolve to forget. He shook his head, imagining the owl flying around with a varmint trap attached to its talons and wondered if anybody would believe his story.

As he sped up the incline on Highway 20 outside Coupeville a patch of blue sky opened in the fog but was quickly covered again. He thought about water-skiing and this took his mind off of the owl and settled him down. Another blue patch opened above him and he drummed on the steering wheel to the music. And then it happened, out of this blue opening in the fog, the decidedly bizarre and absolutely surreal synchronized and became one. Like something out of the Twilight Zone, the owl plunged toward the windshield, the trap still attached to its talon. The shock, the absurdity, and the startling reaction to being dive-bombed caused him to duck. The metal trap crashed against the windshield, shattering it into a thousand tooth-sized aquamarine shards, spraying him and causing him to swerve into the guardrail, flipping and rolling the El Camino and throwing him out of the car into deep grass.

He sat up stunned and noticed the trap lying next to him. He looked up and saw the owl perched on an old oak, staring down at him. He lifted the chain and trap up and shook it at the owl. It flew away into the fog, leaving him in shock, wondering if it was all just a dream. He walked back to the El Camino that was righted on all four wheels and seemed to be in good condition except for the shattered windshield. He opened the door and started it up, and he pulled it back onto the highway, brushing shards of glass off the dash-board. The sun suddenly blasted through the fog and, in no time, burned it all off, leaving a world of golden light and blue skies. He drove home, knowing no one would ever believe his story.

A STORY OF RAPE

Black pools with dead mosquitoes floating on them. They were brackish and had the smell of moth balls. She turned slowly, taking in the devastation that surrounded her. The pools of oil from the trucks and tractors they had used. A two-thousand-square-foot area cleared of all first-growth forest and everything else. Upturned and still planted stumps the size of cookhouse kitchen tables. If you looked at it from above, it appeared to be a square earthen black hole surrounded by the greenest, richest veldt imaginable. The earth she now stepped on had probably not seen the sun for hundreds of years. It made her recall Chief Sealth's historic incantation as he explained this holy land to the conquering white man: "Every part of this soil is sacred in the estimation of my people. Every hillside, every valley, every plain and grove have been hallowed by some sad or happy event in days long vanished."

89

'He got the vanishing part right,' she thought, still surveying the atrocity. She was not only a Park Ranger, but also half Duwamish Indian, like the late great Chief Sealth, so this rape was harsh. The result of the greed of man, logging pirates who would trespass on National Forest and decimate chunks of National Park for financial gain. She estimated the logs taken from this patch would bring in over a quarter of a million dollars on the black market. She felt sick to her stomach. There was no stopping them, the forest so expansive and the number of rangers watching them so minimal.

She looked at her reflection in a black pool, brushed back her hair behind her ear, lifted her hazel eyes, and blew a small spurt of air out. The place smelled like moth balls. She could not shake that smell. Bending down closer to the pool she was looking into, she touched the black water, stirring it, then tasted the liquid from her finger. She spat several times ridding herself of the taste of the polluted boil. She had hiked the five miles up the temporary service road the pirates had used. She figured they had used five trucks. It was a monstrous job that in its dimension would seem almost impossible to get away with, but they did. This was the fifth such clearing that rangers had found in seven years in the Olympic National Park rainforest, the second one she had discovered.

She kicked the dirt and walked to the middle of the cut-out. There she lay on a stump that easily contained her five-foot-five-inch frame. She gazed up at the blue sky, feeling the hard freshly cut stump against her body. She thought about this tree, well over two hundred years old, gone forever now. 'How could people do this?' she wondered. She rolled over and put her cheek against the pitchy wood, trying to divine something from it. An emptiness filled her and then a feeling that she was being watched, so she sat up and looked around and spotted three deer stepping out of the forest into the barrenness, then stopping, frozen like statues.

She studied them curiously, wondering what they were doing. She whistled loudly but they did not move. She stood and walked toward them, yelling at them, but they still did not move. When she got to them she found them inanimate, breathing but with eyes glazed as if they were frozen from fear. Finally she spanked one of them on the haunches and it reared up and gazelled into the forest, snorting. She did the same to the other two with the same result. She watched them disappear into the darkness of the vast forest, marveling at the degree of the effect the clearcut had on the deer.

She shook her head and walked slowly back to her stump in the middle of the devastation. Halfway there the static of her radio interrupted her walk. She took it out of her belted holster.

"Hey Ray, Diedre here. Over." She talked into the walkie-talkie.

"Diedre, how are you doing? Over."

"I found it Ray." Diedre cut off.

There was a silence. "How bad is it?"

Diedre looked around at the stumps the branches and the dirt. "Bad," she sighed.

"Where are you? Over."

"Five miles up from access road X31. Over."

"I'll be there in about an hour. Stay put. Look for evidence. Over."

"Ten-four. Over." Diedre put the radio back in its holster. She hadn't even started to comb the space for evidence. It seemed worthless. They had never found anything before. It seemed quite clear that the people who did this kind of crime were quite professional. But she would have to search anyway. She decided to start at the stump and triangulate from there. She fanned out to each corner looking down at her feet, kicking suspicious mounds of dirt that might be concealing something. After ten minutes of looking, fortune struck when she found a wallet underneath a dismembered branch. She opened it and found it was stuffed with money, identification, credit cards, business cards. She looked at the picture on a California driver's license, a bearded but shaved-headed man whose name was Tom Ballard, six-foot-two, 280 pounds. There was also one hundred ten dollars, an American Express Gold Card, a Mastercard, a dozen or so business cards and several scraps of paper with phone numbers on them. This was motherlode of evidence. She could not believe her good luck.

She walked back to the stump to further inspect the contents of the wallet, spreading them out on the stump; then she heard the sound of a motor coming towards her. She looked at her watch thinking it might be Ray, but it had only been a half hour since they talked. She looked at the contents of the wallet and started gathering up the artifacts and stuffing them back in as quickly as possible, realizing that if it wasn't Ray, it wasn't good. The closer the engine got, the more recognizable it was an All-Terrain Vehicle or ATV, not a Park Truck.

Then the whine of the engine filled the clearcut space. She looked up to see the driver of the three-wheeled ATV spotting her and not looking friendly. She scrambled to stuff the wallet into her coat pocket and ran for the cover of the forest. As she ran she unsheathed her radio again and clicked it on. "Ray, this is Diedre. Over!" she screamed. Panic raced through her as she heard the piercing engine of the ATV almost upon here. "SOS!" she yelled into the radio seeing the versatile vehicle do a wheelie beside her and try to cut off her path to the forest. The engine whined like a rabid animal. Diedre veered at a sprint hoping to make it to the tree line. But before she made it she heard the shot of a single bullet and froze in her tracks.

"Where you running to, Ranger?"

She did not answer, thinking about escape.

"I think you have something of mine," the driver said as he dismounted his vehicle letting it idle, pointing the gun at her.

She still remained silent.

"I guess I'm just going to have to it take back." He approached her slowly and then with a darting hand grabbed

93

her hair and threw her to the ground. Diedre ate dirt and felt the sudden impact of the man's weight on her. His hands quickly raced over her body finding the wallet in her coat pocket; but he did not stop there, ripping her clothes off. She tried to fight but was overpowered. She felt his hands grab her breast and wrestle her bra off.

"Nice tits. Shit, you're sweet as pie," he moaned, grinding his crotch into her ass. His hands unbuckled her belt and she felt as she was going to suffocate in the cold, dark earth. He turned her around toward him and tore her pants down to her knees and ripped her panties off her with the ferocity of a wild animal. As he reached between her legs, she was able to bite him on the shoulder and scratch his eyes, releasing her from his hold. She tried to scramble up but was tripped by her pants and he tried to mount her again but not before she was able to unleash a two-legged kick to his groin. He went down with a huge gasp and she scrambled up, kicking her boots off and tearing her pants off as she sprinted to the woods.

Before she got to the forest line, she heard a bullet but did not stop, instead she zig-zagged the last ten yards into the forest. She ran naked and scared through the green veldt not looking back just running for her life. She did not hear him coming. She did not feel him hit her.

Ray found her lifeless body several hours later, lying on her back beside a tree, eyes open wide and staring at the sky.

GRUNGE REDUX

"What a high!" It had made him forget everything else. She seemed to, also.

The light was breaking over the Cascade Mountains, Seattle skyline still lit in the dark. They sat in the beat-up Jeep sat at the Alki Beach parking lot, a bag full of money between them.

"Yeah!" Nina darted her dark eyes, took a drag from her cigarette, and pressed her lithe body deeper into the worn leather bucket seat.

Fitz opened the window and looked at the oncoming morning light.

Nina opened her window and flicked her cigarette into the wet green.

As Fitz watched her, the inkling of doubt that he had been feeling about their relationship crept into his mind. She had been acting strange lately.

"Let's go for a walk. I'm tired of being in here." Nina opened the door and climbed out.

"Wait." Fitz took the pistol from the glove compartment.

"What are you taking that for?" She looked at him, disgusted. "You aren't going to shoot anyone, are you?"

"I could have shot someone." Fitz climbed out of the Jeep, shut the door, and spun the cylinder of the antiquated six-shooter. There were three bullets left in it.

"You shot it straight up into the sky. If it fell to the ground and struck someone, then maybe you might have shot someone. Otherwise, no way, diddle-ray." Nina walked ahead toward the water.

He lit a cigarette and followed her, stuffing the pistol into his jeans. He admired her fine ass as she sauntered to the sand and then to the water of Elliott Bay. Driftwood from high tide lay like fallen bodies along the beach. What was it with her? It was definitely not good. It could be the end. They had been married for three years, hooking up two years after they graduated from high school. People said they were crazy. Fitz tried to comprehend how crazy it was. Eighteen years old wasn't a real good thinking year. It was a mistake, no one's fault, just a mistake of living a grunge life. And the irony of it all was that the ending would be like this, after a scheme hooked directly to the music and grunge life where they had met.

They had been living off schemes, cons, and small-time crime since they were married, and they had done all right by it; but this was by far was the most profitable deal of them all: selling the shotgun used to kill himself. It was pure genius, Fitz thought, even believing the con himself some of the time. But now that it was done and they had scored, he was back to sad times thinking about what she was about to tell him, how they had gone south, sour, around the bend. They just weren't clicking like they used to. He knew it to be true. They would split the take and part ways.

He shook his head, spied a stick, picked it up, and dragged it behind him. He listened to the water gently lapping at the beach, watched the morning light caterpillaring across the scene. He stopped and breathed a lungfull of salty brine clean air. And he snickered again about the deal they had just pulled off. He had gotten the Remington M11 20-gauge shotgun from a wastoid he was selling heroin to. The shit he sold was pretty bad, cut to nothing; it might as well be a placebo. Anyway, the doper had no money and he proceeded to bring out the shotgun and told the story about what it was and how he had come to be in possession of it. The funny thing was that it sounded more than plausible and made Fitz half believe to the point of taking the gun in exchange for his sub-par horse. The shotgun alone was worth more than the drugs, and the story was absolutely priceless.

The junky had told the story of an electrician who was working at the Cobain house who actually found Kurt dead and reported the death to the police. Well, when the police arrived the shotgun was gone although it was obvious that he had shot himself, and the electrician reported that he had discovered the scene when he looked in a window and he swore that the shotgun was there. The police covered this up because they had so spoiled the crime scene when they broke through French doors and sprayed broken glass all over the room with some shards actually sticking into Cobain's putrefied body. This is why the gun was never seen personally and ended up being destroyed at the request of Courtney Love.

This cover-up would serve to keep whoever did steal the gun from collecting any type of financial gain. Anyway, the doper filled in the gaps by telling Fitz that he had lived down the street from Cobain on Lake Washington Boulevard and explained that he was forever breaking into the Cobain's house mostly just to hang where Kurt hung. He'd sit in the chairs but not harm anything. On that very day, he had wandered into the house and found Kurt dead. He couldn't believe it, and feeling guilty by association, he had fled the scene; but not before he took the gun for his own personal souvenir of the tragedy. He said that he had tried to sell it but nobody believed him. He said he had even written to Courtney several times but she had never written back. He also said he felt a curse from the gun and traced it to his slow death by heroin. But he swore on his black junky heart that this was the real deal suicide weapon, killer of the great Kurt Cobain.

Since then Fitz had checked out the story and, for intents and purposes, it held up. The gun had reportedly been passed to a charitable society from Love, then back to the police, and finally destroyed. But the only thing that had really been passed was paperwork, and the gun never saw the light of day. It could be, Fitz thought, and went about starting a conspiracy theory on the internet, working over a year to create contacts and spread the story of his property, and finally getting some interest from a collector and an offer for twenty-five thousand dollars "upon substantiation." Substantiation was basically verification of the serial number of the shotgun so that it matched the serial number of the gun that Cobain had bought two days before his death. Upon hearing the terms, Fitz had done his own investigating and found out what the serial number was. They weren't the same. So Fitz had a biker friend of his perform his best imitation of a Remington serial number forgery. It never looked quite right to him owing to how many numbers had to be changed. So he was on his own. It was either back out or bluff and maybe even get lucky, as they had.

Nina sat on a tree-length piece of driftwood looking at Puget Sound and the Seattle skyline twinkling across Elliott Bay, her chin in her hands. The light struck her, highlighting her beauty, her long black hair, her slight body and firm breasts that pressed her t-shirt up. She wore no bra. Fitz felt a twinge of desire that slowly turned to frustration the closer he came to her. He looked at the feline tattoo that ran up her shoulder to the side of her neck. They had tattooed themselves and pierced themselves many times together. Each had eight tattoos adorning different parts of their bodies. They had actually made some money tattooing friends and other riff-raff.

Fitz walked up to her, pacing around her, using the stick as a sword, cutting the air in front of him. He looked at Nina and wondered what she was thinking, his slashes with the stick making a wicked air-cutting sound. Nina never looked up, just stared at the water and the sun beginning to rise slowly over the Cascade Mountains.

"I'm sorry." Fitz sighed, defenseless against her silence.

"For what?" She finally looked at him.

"Last night...." He threw the stick in the water and the whole scenario from the night before played out in his head. With balls of steel he had met the perspective buyers at a rendezvous on Lake Washington in a park not a quarter of a mile away from where Cobain had shot himself. The night was dark as coal. They were waiting when he arrived. He had the shotgun wrapped in a pink baby blanket. He stepped out of the Jeep nervous as hell, with Nina in the driver's seat keeping it idling. He approached the BMW where three men in suits sat. That was weird to begin with. He tapped on the window and they all opened their doors simultaneously making Fitz even less comfortable.

"Do you have the gun?" the shortest of the men asked, ignoring formalities.

Unfazed and feeling a bit brave from the Jack Daniel buzz that was sliding up his back from the hit he had taken before he had climbed out of the Jeep, he answered sarcastically, "No, this is a Mastodon's cock. You got the money?"

The short guy nodded to his companion and a bag was taken out of the car and thrown in front of Fitz unceremoniously. Fitz stepped forward and rummaged through the bag. It looked like twenty-five thousand dollars to him. The little guy snapped his fingers and pointed toward the wrapped gun. Fitz handed it to him tenuously. He thought about grabbing the bag and running, but he stood his ground instead, hoping against hope that the forgery would pass. The diminutive one turned the gun in his hands and checked the serial number, rubbing it with his thumb several times, making Fitz more nervous.

"It appears to be real," he said, as he looked down the sights of the shotgun at Fitz.

"Appearances are everything. See ya," Fitz grabbed the bag and headed for the Jeep where Nina waited with engine running.

"Hey wait a minute," one of the men yelled from behind.

But Fitz did not wait. He ran as fast as he could for the Jeep where Nina smartly put on the high beams blinding the threesome, and throwing off the aim of one of them who fired a single shot.

Fitz, hearing this before jumping in the Jeep, took out his six shooter and shot in the sky causing the three men to duck and allowing him to get in and Nina to speed away. They had driven to Capitol Hill, then got on I-5 and just drove for hours running on Jack Daniel's adrenaline and some crystal meth he had found in the Jeep from another high time. They made sure they weren't being followed, but

101

with their paranoia it took a tank of gas until they finally ended up at the Alki Beach parking lot.

"Why are you sorry? We got the money," Nina finally answered.

"I know, but I don't know. What next?" Fitz asked, wanting to get to the point of splitting the money and then splitting, period.

"How about having a baby?" Nina did not look up. In fact, she closed her eyes as she said it.

"What?" Fitz said, the blindside not yet sinking in.

"I'm late. I'm never late."

"What?" Fitz shook his head in disbelief, realizing all that he thought was rejection was really this....

"Three months late." She nodded slowly. "I want to keep it." She covered her face.

Fitz did not speak. He looked out at the brightening bay and a sparkle caught his eyes by the water. He walked toward it without thinking and bent down to pick it up. He grasped the stone and rubbed the sand away. It was an arrowhead, carved to perfection out of a flint or obsidian without any sign of deterioration. The point was still sharp. An excitement ran through him. How could this get him so excited after the night and morning he was having, he wondered?

"Look!" He held the arrowhead towards Nina. "It's an arrowhead." He handed it to Nina who took it, stroked it, and then threw it in the sand.

"What are you doing?" Fitz scrambled to retrieve it. "It's a real Indian arrowhead!"

"I don't care if it's the real shotgun that killed Cobain!" she screamed and walked away, more than making her point.

"Fuck!" Fitz picked up the arrowhead, feeling the metal pain from his piercings in his eye brow and ears, and feeling his anger rising. "Nina!" He ran after her and cut her off, grabbed her shoulders and shook her. "Nina, we should be fucking happy. We got twenty-five thousand dollars and you're going to have a baby!" he said, convincingly. It wasn't such a bad idea, he thought. It was better than her splitting on him.

"I can't have a baby." Nina shook her head, surprised by his willingness.

"Why not? We got financial means. We could open a tattoo and piercing shop." Fitz said it with conviction.

"It's not that." She picked up a stone and threw it into the water. The ripples slowly headed out to sea on a silent, slow wave.

"What then?"

"Shit, Fitz, with all the drugs you and I have put in our bodies for the last five years, the baby would probably have a foot coming out its head."

That made Fitz laugh which made her mad. He put the arrowhead in his pocket.

"It would!" she cried and turned her back on him.

Fitz put his arm on her shoulders and drew himself close to her multi-pierced ear and whispered, "Don't hurt yourself. I want some help to help myself. She's just as bored as me, I have this friend, you see, who makes me feel, I don't

103

regret a thing...." He was repeating Nirvana lyrics that he didn't remember memorizing.

She turned to him, tears filling her eyes, kissed him passionately, took his hand, and walked with him into the prune-colored water; and they swam away from shore, together....

TOMMY BASEBALL

Tommy McGee grew up in Mukilteo, Washington, not far from the ferry docks that transported people back and forth from Whidbey Island on a daily basis so that these island people could commute to Everett, Seattle, and all points sprawl. He was a natural. He played baseball like a magician from the time he was six years old. As a kid he played with the older boys in what was called The Ditch, an old abandoned gravel pit that some baseball enthusiasts had cleaned and turned into a crude dirt baseball diamond. Instead of fences for home runs it had the cliffs of the dig. If you hit it onto the cliff it was a home run and was thrown back by someone who was usually watching from above. The cliffs, just about eight feet high, were also the grandstands.

The kids played there all day during the summer and sometimes into night when parents would park their cars and turn their headlights on, all for the sake of finishing the game. Baseball was serious business. When Tommy started playing, parents came to see his acrobatics at second base and his uncanny batting eye. His mother never watched him, but his dad who had pitched semi-pro for the Bellingham Bells, had him dodging fastballs at three. He worked at the Boeing plant but worked as just hard on Tommy's game, setting up a hitting net and a pitchback in the backyard. Mrs. McGee was a cheerful woman who always had an apron on and, although she didn't really approve of having fastballs thrown at her three-year-old baby, when she saw him foul off a couple and then slam a line drive precipitously near her husband's groin, she learned to live with it.

Tommy's feats in The Ditch became legend His double plays were unchoreographed ballet, his throws like a slingshot, and his quickness like a spider monkey. One time when he was eight, the right fielder had to go home early so Tommy played both second base and right field and on one play he ran from second to the right field cliff and robbed Dirk Bellows of a home run. And then on the next play he laid out flat snagging a line drive by Brian Drake and finished the unassisted double play by standing and sprinting to first base, outrunning the leading-off-and-untagged-up Tony Greer. It was miraculous. And all the boys he played with were four and five years older. His hitting was even more spectacular, an art unto itself. In one game he had twenty-six rbi's, going seven for seven with three home runs—two of which were grand slams—two automatic doubles, and two triples. On one of the triples, the first base coach John Eychaner tried to stop him from going past first so that he could officially hit for the circuit, but he couldn't stop Tommy.

He did everything. He stole bases, pulled baseballs out of the gravel dirt like diamonds, and perfected the look-what-I-found. His glove work was sublime. Once an unassisted triple play turned into a family feud on second base when Tommy dove to catch yet another line drive hit by Garry Lange, tagged out his bother Ron Lange who was running to second, and then ran to touch second base to force an untagged-up Steve Lange. The brothers brawled on second base blaming each other for the disaster. Dream-player Tommy McGee was becoming a legend. When he was ten, the high school coach Gene Verburg wanted him to play for him but league rules would not allow it although it was quite well known that Coach Verburg acquired a fake birth certificate for him.

Tommy was five foot, eight inches tall when he entered junior high, tall for his age with more coming. His hands were huge which accounted for his great glove work and bat handling. He was a good-looking kid with dimples in both cheeks. His hair was an unkempt red, never brushed but by a hand. His dad cut his hair, so it never was even. His eyes were as blue as robins' eggs. He never talked much unless he talked about baseball and then the floodgates would open and you would start hearing about baseball history and the debate about who was the greatest player, team, and of course second baseman. Robbie Alomar was his hero and he compared him to the greatest in history. He wanted to be there.

He wanted to be and was going be the greatest second baseman ever to play the game.

In his three years on the junior high baseball team he led the team to three championships. Other coaches in the league gawked at his abilities, and by the time he was in ninth grade there were always rumors that there were college coaches in the crowd, not to mention big league scouts. When he finally made it to high school, a much-anticipated state championship was being conceived possible by Coach Verburg. Tommy led off and batted .426, led the league in stolen bases and was second in home runs. Unfortunately the team was not quite as skilled and they ended up in third place with a 9-8 record. But better times were coming. All were counting on that, and they were right.

His junior year was one of greatness. He batted .450, led the league in every offensive statistic recorded—home runs, doubles, walks, steals, even hit-by-pitches. He led the team to the state championships when some bad luck ended the run but still gave Mukilteo a third-place finish at state, the best in their history. And Tommy was all-state, all-nation, all-universe. Big league scouts were begging him to go pro. His father was being wined and dined by the Mariners, Yankees, and Cardinals. His mother was talking to colleges who were interested in giving him full scholarships. Everyone in town knew who he was and treated him like a hero. And for Tommy's part, he was gracious hero. He knew what he was and performed the necessary home-town hero politics naturally.

One day in the summer between his junior and senior year, Tommy was down at the old rock quarry throwing rocks at a can that floated in the clear water thinking about what to do, go pro or go to college. Tommy hit the can seven out of ten times, the chime of aluminum bouncing off the sheer stone cliffs of the quarry. Clint Ditmar and Ned Soakes were smoking a cigarette they had found on the ground when they hiked up. They coughed deliriously with each toke they took, their virgin lungs rejecting the poison. They offered it to Tommy who waved it off. He continued to throw at the floating can, making the decision in his mind if he hit the can ten times straight he would go pro. He bent down picking the best throwing rocks, setting them aside. He ran his count to eight straight, but he didn't like the last two rocks he had set aside. He searched and found a projectile that he did not recognize. It was not a rock, but he picked it up. It was of perfect throwing weight, but it was metal. As he wound up to throw, it the ancient detonation of a left-behind blasting cap exploded, blowing off half of his arm and his ear. The blasting cap, left untouched for over ten years, triggered the end of a baseball legend.

Next newsworthy thing you would hear about Tommy was six years later when he was arrested for disturbing the peace, vandalism, breaking and entering, possession of stolen property, and resisting arrest. It seems Tommy had gotten drunk, which is how he spent most of his days, and had broken into the high school and stolen a bag of baseballs and a fungo bat. He had taken the stolen property downtown and climbed a fire escape and started hitting the balls left handed breaking windows, street lights and car windshields at three o'clock in the morning. The police tried to get him down but he held them off with a vicious left handed swing and line drive batted hard balls. He actually broke the ribs of one of the cops. He was finally subdued crying in a near nervous breakdown and spent the night in jail.

Judge Hub Clay oversaw the case, a fan of Tommy's in years past. He sentenced him to public service not only coaching a little league team but keeping the two little league baseball diamonds in town in playing shape. Tommy performed his duties with aplomb and soon coached the Twins to a championship and took them to state where they finished third. That was in Tacoma, Washington. After the game Tommy just sat in the dugout as his players marched by. He congratulated them and gave them each a piece of Bazooka. He never got on the bus, telling people he was going to visit some friends. But he never returned to Mukilteo, the home of his heroics. His car was found in a mud flat in Port Ludlow having careened off the road and plunging forty feet down a cliff into the mud of the Puget Sound. It landed nose first and stayed exactly like that. The car could not be removed, so it remains slowly rusting away. Tommy died instantly on impact.

Next significant news about Tommy McGee was that his father was arrested in Seattle at Safeco Field caught sprinkling ashes around second base. In years since he has been arrested at Yankee Stadium and Fenway Park doing the same thing.

SACRED SALMON

D on, his father, stared out the window with the usual sadness scribbled all over his face. A wrinkle twitched on his forehead; it twitched again. At 82 he still looked good—lean body, bald head, and ice blue eyes. He was his dad but more of a friend, his fishing partner, the man who had taught him how to fish. His dad turned slowly toward him and talked in his slow monotone voice. "What d'ya think? Think it's gonna to rain? The fish will be up if it rains. Maybe we should go fishing."

"Well, rain is always a possibility, Dad. Didn't you make up the saying that if you could see Mt. Rainier, it was going to rain, and if you couldn't see Rainier, it was already raining." He chuckled at the family standard for weather humor.

Don looked out at the grayness. It held the day in the palm of its hand and played with the dullness that lies inhibited in minds. It made everything motionless. "Ya know, I read the most ludicrous thing in the paper about my generation being the great generation according to some book by Tom Brokaw." He cackled upon hearing himself say it.

"You don't think so?"

"The greatest flop generation is more like it. Great for what? Because we fought in a bunch of worthless wars? Great generations don't fight in wars. They wage peace. Great generations don't create weapons of mass destruction. Great generations don't waste most of the world's natural resources in the short time they inhabit this planet. A great big fat flop is all I can say for my generation. It'll be better when we're all dead in the earth nourishing the soil instead of sucking it dry."

"Don't die of a heart attack on me," he said trying to calm the tirade of which is father was well known. "Besides, I thought you were proud of your service. Didn't you win the Distinguished Service Medal?" he asked, knowing quite well he had.

"If I had any honor, I would have given that to charity, or melted it down and returned it to the earth. The military and war are the most worthless of human endeavors. You kill someone because you're ordered to, not knowing who you're killing and usually not knowing why; but you're doing it because some cuss is ordering you to. Can you imagine millions of people killed because someone ordered someone else to do it? I mean, if anybody had half a brain the whole concept of war would be laughed off the planet. And these people you are taking orders from are the full-fledged members of cult of death. They will try to convince you they are doing it for the common good and wrap it up in a big colorful patriotic package of brain-washing, and you know what? People believe it. We're all fools led by the worst and most evil."

"Wow, Dad, you're on a roll. Maybe we should go fishing?"

"Fishing?" Don looked out his six-foot-by-six-foot picture window at the weather again. He scratched his head. "Where?"

"The Hole, Deception Pass. I know there's a king salmon waiting for me today."

"You think so? A king. I heard they're running, but ah, why not? Get the gear. The boat's hooked up," Don said, and he smiled, forgetting about the greatest generation for a second. He stood in his old man fashion, creaking, groaning and finally lifting himself to a stand. "It's easier to die than to stand these days."

"You okay?" He walked toward him to steady him but stopped midway.

"Yeah go get the ice chest and the gear. Let's go. I got the feeling in me. We're going to catch a big one. Giddy-up boy." His father seemed to rise off the floor flush with excitement.

He walked out the door in a hurry, excited by the levitation of his father. It was fifteen-foot boat with a 500-horsepower outboard Evinrude motor. It was beige and showing the wear of being used steadily for over fifteen years. He checked the poles land checked the tackle box to see there were enough weights, extra line, and hooks. He noticed three squid lures and five spasm metallic spinners. They would stop by Cornet Bay Marina for some herring. He put the ice chest with a half case of Budweiser and a bottle of water in it on the back seat of the boat. They would buy a sandwich at the marina. He backed the boat out of the driveway and honked the horn.

Don walked out of the house with his waders on, smoking a cigarette and wearing his thread-worn lucky fishing hat with Similk Beach Golf Course emblazoned on it. He climbed into the truck, slammed his door, and said, "Let's go catch us a sacred salmon, Son." He often used the description sacred when he spoke of salmon to his reverence of the fish and fishing ritual.

They took the back road from Anacortes along Madrona Point, Dugualla Bay and Rosario Beach arriving at Highway 20 at Pass Lake. The road snaked up the glacier-hewn cliffs to Deception Pass Bridge that hovered a hundred feet over The Hole. Deception Pass was a formidable navigational waterway with currents that changed with the tides that ran with such ferocity that if your boat was not up to it, you were stranded on one side of the pass until slack tide or the tide was with you. On the southern side of the pass close to the northerly most point of Whidbey Island where the currents were the strongest and usually whirlpools formed from the tides was The Hole where, on any given fishing day, you could see boats being spun by the constantly turning eddies and current. The Hole was the feeding and resting place for salmon as they went through Deception Pass into the mouth of the Skagit River before going upstream to spawn and die. The Hole was renowned for the king salmon that were caught there, the biggest being a sixty-two-pound behemoth by some tourist (which always pissed his father off).

Not that they had not caught their fair share.

As they drove across the bridge, his father lifted up in his seat and looked down at the hole. "One boat is all I see," he said and then settled down. "Slack tide in two hours. Tide is going out. We're in luck," Don said as he took an old tarnished flask from his fishing jacket, unscrewed the top, and took a sip of unadulterated Canadian whiskey. He offered some to his son who shook it off. They arrived in the tranquil Cornet Bay and went directly to the marina where they bought herring and sandwiches.

He skillfully backed the boat down into the water, being directed by his father, and then he parked the truck in the parking lot and hurried back his dad already at the controls. As Don revved the Evinrude, he walked gingerly into the briny cold bay water, the floor all barnacled rocks and mud. He jumped onto the bow of the boat and tight-roped to the passenger seat. Don put the boat in gear and it dug into the water and forcefully pushed ahead leaving a deep wake.

The whited water churned and Don made a beeline to the channel between Whidbey and Deer Islands, and then turned the corner into the strait. The view was muted by the fog but still spectacular. The outgoing tide helped them

115

speed toward The Hole. They traveled twenty yards from the shore that was no shore at all, just sheer rock cliffs that rose up with crags of first growth Douglas fir and cedar spotting the rocks. Salt water sprayed them from the bow as they got closer, not saying anything, the day still as gray as ash. A wet chill hung in the air with patches like ghosts being released from the crannies in the cliffs. When they were directly under the bridge, Don put the boat on idle and they went to work baiting their hooks. About a hundred feet away, another boat hovered in the middle of The Hole, large whirlpools surrounding it. Two fishermen watched their poles and talked about the currents. They nodded a hello to them.

He was first in the water with his skewered herring. Don steered the boat, then cast toward the shore. And they both grabbed a beer from the cooler.

"I wonder if they got anything over there," he asked, cracking open his Budweiser.

Don looked over at the other boat slowly circling around the whirlpool. "Naw," he said, and as he did one of the men in the other boat got a strike. They watched as the man ferociously fought the diving fish. "Cod," Don said, knowing the ways of all strikes, and they watched as the man reeled in a large cod, uglier than a warthog. The man who caught it held it happily and Don groaned There was no room for cod in his boat.

His son bit his tongue, not saying how cod was good eating fish and starting the age-old battle with the old man about the sacrosanct salmon compared to all other fish. He snapped his line thinking he felt a strike but it was just the weight being taken by a wild stream. He looked up at Deception Pass Bridge above him, green against the slate sky, the dulled rumble of traffic passing over reaching down to them. He looked at his father sipping his beer and watching his leader. He had seen him age recently and that had scared him; but he still believed that his dad would outlive him. Don had outlived his wife and one daughter, who had died tragically in a car accident at the age of eighteen. Now it was just he and his father on the open seas together. He had been divorced for twenty years and had two daughters who were married, both in California. He usually traveled down to see them once a year. His mother had died five years before of cancer.

"I went over to the old house the other day," his father said, not taking his eye off his line. The old house was the one he had grown up in and one that his dad had sold soon after his mother died. "You know, I heard your mother's voice in my head, clear as a bell. 'Go see the begonias.' The voice was so clear I could swear she was there, but it must just be an echo released from way deep from ancient history. You know, she said those words so often. 'Go see the begonias,'" he repeated.

The begonias being the prize bellweathers she grew in their backyard. It was a kidney- shaped garden filled with the finest soil created by hundreds of pounds of salmon guts. Every salmon that they had ever caught. Begonias are

117

usually annual, but not his mother's. They were gargantuan sun-like begonias that would bloom all spring and summer.

"Don't get me wrong when I say I heard a voice. I'm not going crazy. It's just a voice in me. I'm not starting to lose it like Swede, and if I ever do start losing my mind, not remembering things, you kill me, you hear me? Take me out on this boat and drown me. I'm not going to go out a babbling idiot. Drown me. Do you hear me?"

"I hear you, Dad. I've heard you before." He wondered if he would ever have the nerve to do such a thing. He opened another beer. Did you see them?" he asked.

"What?"

"The begonias?"

"Yeah, like a criminal. No one was there so I climbed the fence and took a look. The yard is a disaster not a stitch of grass left. Chunks of old cars lying around rusting, garbage everywhere. The garden itself is no more, but blooming like cantaloupes are your mother's begonias among all the garbage. Quite amazing. If she was alive she'd probably die seeing the place, but it would make her happy to see those flowers still surviving the worst of it."

The sudden whir of his line being taken silenced Don who stood jerking the pole and setting the hook. Don reeled in the line and played with the fish. As he brought it close to the surface, the silver sheen of a salmon sparkled in the green water. He got the net ready and, as the fish dove under the boat, his father followed it, walking his pole to the otherside. Don yanked the line and the fish surfaced; he lowered the net and nabbed the fish. Not a king salmon but a silver weighing in at about fifteen pounds. His dad dragged his hand along the sleek smooth body. "Nope, you're not the fish we came for," he said, deftly unhooking the fish and raising the fish up to show the other fishermen who were now paying attention. He lowered it down to the water and freed the salmon. "That'll piss off those cod catchers." He laughed while he tended to his hook, skewering another herring. "First fish, I think that means you're either buying or cooking dinner."

"It won't be the first time," he said, setting his mind to catching a fish now. His father was renown for releasing more salmon than most people caught. Once when there were three in the boat, he and Swede and his dad, his dad caught everyone's limit, nine kings each weighing near thirty pounds. It was amazing. They smoked all those salmon in an old refrigerator his dad had converted into a smoker. They ate smoked salmon every winter all winter. During the summer they would bake, barbecue, and saute salmon weekly. One thing he did have growing up was plenty of omega oil.

"How's the job?" His dad asked him as he slowly let out his line and brought the boat about simultaneously.

"Samo-samo, digging a ditch is digging a ditch," he answered. He was a backhoe operator for the state out of Anacortes a job he had held for thirty years. "A couple more years is all I got in me," he said, feeling another tug on his line and then, seizing the initiative, he jerked the pole and

119

felt the wane of his line.

"What do ya got?" Don asked looking over his shoulder.

"Seaweed," he said, reeling in the dead weight that bent his pole down towards the water. He untangled the kelp and put a fresh herring on his hook. He stood up and gave a medium cast toward the cliffs and then sat back down and sipped on his beer. "Want a sandwich?" he asked, as he unwrapped his ham and cheese from the plastic container.

"Sure." His dad took his and they ate slowly, drinking their beers and watching their lines as the boat slowly trolled in a circle around The Hole staying always a hundred yards or more from the other boat. After about forty-five minutes of fishing and getting no hits, his dad reeled in his line and switched from herring to a shimmering lure. "Maybe this will get their attention," he said, as he cast the shiny metal spinner towards the middle of The Hole.

They drifted slowly in circles for an hour making small talk about the amazing Mariners who were tearing up the league. He tried to talk his dad into going to California to visit his granddaughters and great-grandchildren, to no avail. His dad didn't like traveling; he didn't like leaving his house except to fish. The gray day still loomed with no precipitation. The other boat drifted away from The Hole and then headed out toward Rosario Beach, impatient with the fishless lull. Slack tide arrived and the engine puttered them around in circles, their lines both drifting back, tight in the troll. They changed bait and changed bait again, but still they did not even have a bite. They both lingered in the reverie of mind-wandering fishing. Then Don heard it, clear as bell, his wife's voice again, murmuring another of her much-said phrases, "Catch a big one." It was so clear he looked around the boat coming eye to eye with his son.

"I heard it." His son said, astonished, "Did you hear that?"

"What ?" his father asked, not wanting to project senility.

"Mom, she just said 'catch a big one.'" He shook his head. "Did you hear it?" he asked his dad again, dumbfounded.

"Yes, I did. You heard those words, 'catch a big one'?" his dad asked in disbelief.

"Yes!" he said, looking around curiously, and as he spoke both their poles were struck and their lines whined and their reels spun recklessly. Both amazed and amused, they went to work with quick pops setting their hooks and reeling like mad men. Both fish fought with ferocity pulling the boat into the middle of the Pass away from The Hole. A half hour later they both had landed their fish, a pair of almost identical thirty-pound king salmon. They could not believe what had happened or how to explain it, but nothing could express the excitement they felt. More excited than when either caught their first fish. The witnessed event of hearing her voice and both catching the 'big one' made them both giddy and it is all they talked about all the way back to his father's house where they prepared the fish for dinner. They barbecued one and froze the other. His father set a place for his mother as an appropriate appreciation of the magical, and they ate sacred salmon steaks with salad and baked potatoes, musing about the miraculous.

BETWEEN THE MAD
AND THE MUNDANE

She stared straight into the television set, not watching, the TV light flickering, nibbling at her fingernails, but not biting them, once in while pulling some popcorn from the near-empty wooden bowl, eating each kernel slowly, peeling each fluff, nibbling on the lightly buttered corn, taking forever. It drove some people she knew insane, but this is the way she liked to eat it, letting it melt in her mouth piece by piece. She had eaten almost a whole bowl of popcorn like this. Now she was in a daze, feeling full.

A rainy Sunday in Seattle. She had had lunch with Jill from the office who depressed her to no end. Jill was married and having problems. What lawyers don't have marital problems? It came with the territory; in fact, it was part of the bylaws. That's why she never got married, that and time. She had been a lawyer for twelve years and she seemed to have no time at all except on this dreary Sunday.

Nothing was on TV. She threw a kernel of popcorn at the screen on that thought alone. It should be ashamed of itself, she thought. How could such a magnificent technology be so mediocre, barely? Whitey had this whole theory about why everything was so mediocre and why it was going to get better. Something about all the people who are running things now were born in the late thirties and early forties, being poorly nourished because of the lack of nutrients during the depression and war. Their mental functions had been dwarfed to only imagine mediocrity. The mediocre generation. The baby boom generation of the fifties and sixties had been weaned on the best the world could offer in the post-war times of good, pure, and plenty, and so they were more highly evolved. And finally children from the generation of the seventies and eighties, his generation, would be the first true 'chemical children,' because of the additives in almost every food group, even mother's milk. When the depression generation runs its course the mediocrity will end. Whitey made the scariest sense sometimes. He was way too smart for his own good.

Liz sat up, then stood, tossing the last couple of popcorn kernels into the bowl. She picked up the bowl and carried it to the kitchen. She put it in the sink, ran warm water over her greasy hands, took a paper towel and dried them. She opened the doors under the sink and threw the damp paper towel in the garbage can. Two flies flew out like kamikazes making her jump back and muffle a scream. Mad at herself for being startled by mere flies, she grabbed a can of insecticide and sprayed them relentlessly until she had emptied the half-full can. She started to cough from ingesting the spray and watched as the flies fell from mid-air and bounced on the linoleum. She picked them up by the wings and threw them into the garbage. "Serves you right, you flying pestilence. Don't mess with me."

She ran water over her hands again but this time just wiped them on her pants and walked out of the kitchen escaping the reek of the spray.

She picked up the postcard Whitey had sent her from school; at least she thought he had sent it from school. It was a picture of an Alaskan, Oomingmak, and a type of ox that Eskimos raise on co-op farms for their underwool, called Qiviut. They made scarves, hats, and other clothing from it. She had a hat made of it. 'There is nothing finer or warmer than Qiviut wool,' Whitey would preach.

The thing was her brother was supposed to be in college at Evergreen. Why was this a post card from Alaska? She checked the postmark to confirm her suspicions. He was in Alaska again. She read the scrawl: 'Elizabeth, I'm here, please come and visit me. From your emulating, admiring and loving brother, Whitey. P.S. You can't say no to these ox eyes.'

She laughed at that. Her brother always made her happy, but he always irritated her, too. She had not seen him in a while so she suspected he had gone on another quest. 'The quest to leave behind mundaneness' is how he described it. Ever since he had started college, at sixteen, life had just been a romp up and down the west coast for him. He had graduated with a degree in computer science in two years and was now getting his Masters. He was a genius.

They had lived together for one year on their own after their mother died in a car accident. Their father had died five years earlier of cancer. There were only the two of them left. Two Leggetts left. She was thirty-six; he was eighteen. A 'pleasant mistake' is how her mother once described him. A perfect albino with white hair that seemed to be pulled toward heaven. He was a crazy genius.

They had both just got used to not having a father and then their mother died. Liz had been on her own, so the death wasn't quite as shocking for her; at least that's what she told herself. Whitey, at fifteen, moved in all calm and collected, used to death, having lived two years with their father's slow cancer. She shuddered at that thought.

They grieved over losing their mother and celebrated finding each other. They bonded that year, and then he went to college with a full academic scholarship in computer science. He could have gone to the University of Washington, MIT, anywhere, but he chose Evergreen State College, a notoriously liberal school about fifty miles south of Seattle. 'It's Evergreen,' he would say, like that was explanation enough. No one could believe it.

Over the last four years he had visited often, always popping in right when she needed him most. Always calling right when she was going to lose it. And always sending quirky post cards from everywhere just to lighten her mood. His sense of timing was miraculous if not magical. He was special.

She picked up the card and stood. And now he wants me just to drop everything and visit him. He must think vacations grow on trees at law offices. What was he doing in Anchorage, anyway? He had worked on some fishing boats up there during the summer and was an apprentice plumber in the Arctic Circle with a friend's dad the summer before that. He liked Alaska almost as much as he liked California, a state he had hitchhiked up and down.

She marveled at all the things her brother had already done. Half her age and twice the worldly experience. She had gone to school and then to more school, had become a lawyer and a partner. She was on the beaten path; he was off it. It made her a little jealous, and a little worried; but what could she do: He was a chemical child; she was a baby boomer, stuck with her high evolution, wishing they had thrown a few more additives into her Gerber's. Maybe then mundaneness wouldn't be something she liked but would be something she made a quest to escape. Yes, between madness and mundaneness, she had chosen the mundane, would choose it any day. Whitey, never.

She jerked up, startled by the doorbell, wondering who in the hell this could be at eleven-thirty at night? She thought about her Louisville Slugger in the closet if this was an intruder. She looked out the peep. It was Sally from down the hall in her night robe. She opened the door still wondering why so late.

127

"Sally," she deadpanned as she opened the door.

"Liz, can I come in?" Sally asked, already walking in. She was short, cute, sweet and sometimes a pain in the ass. She had a pensive, mad look on her face that Elizabeth had never seen before, and she started talking as if in mid-sentence, continuing a conversation. No greetings, just straight to the grief.

"You know what he told me? He told me that he, that he...." Sally searched for the word until it finally exploded in a pop at her lips, "...cheated on me. He just told me that. We'd just got done. Done doing it. And he tells me as calmly as that. He had to clear his conscience. Tells me that a year ago, when he went to Nashville on that shoot for Burger King, he did it. What am I going to do, Liz? I mean I should have known. I remember that trip, his sheepish mood, generous as all hell after it. We've been married five years, Liz? What am I going to do?"

Elizabeth had barely heard any of this; she caught 'cheating' and that's about it. Right as Sally began to talk, the funniest thing happened: an image of her brother popped in her head. Whitey, her albino brother, white hair, blue eyes, standing all six foot four of him with that goofy smile, waving to her, saying, "Come visit me up in Anchorage, Lizzie." He laughed and waved again with his huge hands. Next thing she knows Sally is standing in front of her with this look of give-me-the-meaning-of-life on her face. She tried not to laugh.

"He did tell you," Elizabeth said. "That's something." She looked in the mirror and brushed her hair back, thinking about her brother.

"A year later he tells me! And what if this has happened before? What if this is just to purge a very guilty conscious?" Sally's usually perky voice quivered with a moan.

There was no answer to this, so Elizabeth gave no answer. She looked at this sad woman in front of her, wondering why she had chosen her door to knock on? They were not the closest of friends; they just happened to have lived on the same floor of the same apartment building for the last five years. Elizabeth did not know much more about her and her husband other than they were both in advertising, that she was an account director and he was a writer with aspirations of being a playwright. Not enough information to make them friends. They'd never even shared an evening together.

"What am I going to do, Liz? I can't go back there. Can I stay the night here?" Sally begged.

Elizabeth choked on that and took an unconscious step back, "Well…."

"Oh, thank you, Liz," Sally said, not listening, and then she walked to the couch and bit her nails, breathing through her nose.

Elizabeth stood there in a state of disbelief staring at Sally, wondering about what had just transpired; but before she could go one way or the other, there was a knock on the door.

"That's him. Don't let him in," Sally pleaded.

"Sally, are you in there?" Bill called, his voice smothered by the door.

"Don't let him in, Liz."

Elizabeth's heart churned and her stomach growled. She was still confused. Not listening to Sally, she walked to the door and opened it. Bill walked in, calm, wearing his bathrobe. He walked past Elizabeth to the couch where Sally was sitting.

"I love you, Sally." Bill bent to touch her, but was fought off by Sally's swiping hands.

"Get away! Just get away!" Sally screamed. She stood up, circled around the coffee table away from Bill. "You cheated! You cheated!"

"I know. And I confessed. I feel terrible. I love you. I'm sorry."

"No, no, never. I hate you! I hate you!" Sally cried and ran to the door, opened it, and left, slamming the door as she flew through it.

There was a silence and Elizabeth again tried to make sense out of what was going on. It all happened so fast she did not know whether to be upset or to laugh hysterically, lost in the absurdity of it all. Bill just stood there, bath-robed, his lip quivering, wanting to say something.

"Can you believe that?" He finally uttered, pointing at the closed door.

Elizabeth followed the point and did not say anything, thinking only, Can you believe this? Before she could answer Bill was hugging her, crying on her shoulders. She felt suddenly paralyzed.

"What am I going to do, Liz, what am I going to do?" He cried, holding her tighter and tighter, his beard stubble rubbing against her neck, his skin against her skin. She could smell his breath, his skin, the faint touch of after-shave; and then, out of nowhere, she felt him kiss her twice softly by her right ear. She jerked back holding her hand in front of her, angry.

"Bill, I have a thirty-four-ounce Louisville Slugger in my closet. I'm about to go get it out and land it across your skull."

He did not blink. She did not stir. And just like that Bill was on his knees, laughing, bent over hard and laughing. Suddenly there was another knock on the door. Elizabeth, shell-shocked, walked over and opened it. In walked Sally, not saying anything to Elizabeth, but walking straight over to her hysterical husband.

"What happened, Bill?" Sally asked, standing over him.

"She, she...," Bill tried to talk but could not, laughter spilling from him in waves.

"She what?" Sally said. She grabbed him by the shoulders and shook him.

Bill stood barely calming himself, and finally, in huffs and puffs, said, "It was perfect. Perfect." He walked past Sally, past Elizabeth and out the door.

Elizabeth stood stone stunned, finally realizing it was all an act. There was no reaction she could have in this situation. Nothing to draw on from the past. She had a horrible taste in her mouth.

"Liz, I'm sorry. You see, Bill is writing this play and he couldn't find an ending, and so, well, I hope you understand."

"No, I don't understand," she said, burning holes in all solid matter. "I don't understand at all." Sally blushed when she came in contact with that stare. She hunched and withered to the door. She left apologizing profusely.

Elizabeth chain-locked the door, and walked to the kitchen. She stared at the clock: 1:30 a.m. She shook her head in disgust. She was on the edge of doing something crazy, feeling the rage of being made a fool. She stomped back into the living room in a storm to turn off the television that had been blaring through all of this. The postcard from Whitey caught her eye again. The longhaired Oomingmak, with friendly kind eyes, stood there, staring at her in the most peaceful way. Suddenly she felt calm, relieved.

The phone rang and she went ballistic, swearing that if it was them she was going to rip the phone from the wall and take it to their apartment and stuff it down their throats. She thought about the two flies she had fumigated earlier. The phone rang again, and she went red with rage. She yanked the receiver from its cradle and yelled in utter madness, "Now what??!! What do you want now??!!"

There was a silence, and then a nervous chuckle. "Hi Lizzie," Whitey's voice stopped time. "You okay?"

.

SPACE NEEDLE

1962 was a very big year for Washington State, for Seattle, and for every kid within a five-hundred-mile radius who drove their parents slowly insane by repeating the mantra a zillion or more times: 'Can we go? Can we go? Can we go?' Where they wanted to go was the World's Fair in Seattle, to see the exhibits, ride the monorail, be amused at the amusement park, gorge themselves at the world food court, and, finally and most importantly, go to the top of the Space Needle. I was one of those irritating go-go-go kids, as was everyone else on my block.

Finally, the time that would never come arrived. We piled six kids and two mothers into the Belair and headed south to the thrill of the World's Fair. Nine million six hundred thousand people visited the fair, including Elvis Presley and John F. Kennedy. That day it seemed as if there were a million people crowding the site. My choice of food proved to be a real irritant to my mother. 'Here we are in the world's dining hall, where you can eat food from all over the globe, and all you want is soda, cotton candy, popcorn and hot dogs,' she lamented. I wasn't the only kid who stuck to the standards, but not without having some chow mein, curry, tacos and squeak-and-bubble forced down my throat in small sample spoon-sized bites. Even this forced feeding could not take any of the shine off the day. It was everything it was supposed to be; it was reality living up to expectations. It was a joy ride to the future. Sadly, it to had to end, but not before we all headed for the much-ballyhooed ride up to the top of the Space Needle.

We walked, five kids astride, stained with food, and redfaced with exhaustion and excitement, pulling our mothers to the final destination. But when we got there my reaction was not what I had expected. When I looked up at the hovering disc five hundred feet above, I froze in my tracks. My friends tried to forcibly pull me toward the elevator, but I did not move. My mother tried to coax me with soft words, but I shook uncontrollably. After much convincing, I could not be persuaded to climb into the elevator. I shamedly stayed on the ground, then cried my eyes out from embarrassment while the rest of my friends went up and saw the view that I would be teased for not seeing for the rest of my life. It was even mentioned in the keynote speech at my high school graduation. The Space Needle was pure misery for me, and to torment myself even more, I later attended the University of Washington and then took a job, so the Space Needle gleamed victorious over me wherever I went.

Eventually, we must all face our fears, or take at least an elevator up them. That day came without any desire of my own. I would never go up the big lousy hypodermic tower—that was my lot in life— but a begging six-year-old daughter is hard to argue with. There we were at the Seattle Center checking out the Experimental Music Project and the building designed by Frank Gehry. We went on some rides and she had a cotton candy, and then, out of nowhere she says, "Daddy I want to go up there." She pointed straight up. I looked up at the demon needle.

"You don't want to do that," I explained. "It's much too high and scary." Sweat popped on my brow.

"I like high and scary," she said, finishing her cotton candy and pulling me as only a six-year-old can pull toward the Space Needle from hell, nearly forty years after my first, last, and only encounter with it. I was dumbstruck, but my daughter left me no time to pause, my hand gripped tight by her sticky, hot little fingers. I was on the elevator heading up before I knew what was happening. It was as if I blacked out, and when I came back to consciousness, the door opened and I was on the Observation Deck that slowly turned 360 degrees per hour.

"Look Dad! Look Dad!" she yelled. My daughter couldn't hold back her excitement and I couldn't shake my stunned demeanor. I obeyed her command and looked.

It was an amazing view on a very clear sunny day. Mount Rainier loomed quietly, waiting to someday unleash tons of lava down its glacier fields. The Olympic Mountains shined

135

like crooked white teeth. Elliott Bay pulsated light in full-blown twinkle sheen. Mount Baker pillowed whiteness near the Canadian border. And then the Cascade Mountains, looking like crumbled aluminum foil, stretched north and south as far as the eye could see. It was truly breathtaking. I looked down at my daughter and then leaned down and kissed the top of her head, having a feeling that this was one of those few moments in life you cherish to the grave. I had done it, defeated my fear. What had I been so afraid of, anyway?

When the tower began to shake I thought it was the turning platform grinding a bearing or something. It barely made me flinch, but when it continued and I felt the whole needle roll up and down and up and down in slow motion, my heart stopped. People screamed; plates and glasses crashed to the floor. The shaking continued for what seemed like forever. I picked my daughter up, squeezing her tight with her squeezing me back even tighter. I felt the involuntary evacuation of excrement in my pants. I trembled and started to feel a whimper rise from my stomach. I stopped it by looking at my crying daughter and clenching my teeth and my butt cheeks to stop any other unauthorized bowel movements. I breathed through my nose and focused as I felt the rocking Space Needle begin to slow and then steady.

There was a nervous sigh and a silent but sure heading for the elevators, with whispers of aftershocks in the darkness. The lights blinked back on, but the elevators were not working. We were trapped in the disc with paranoid fears of what might happen next. It was the biggest earthquake to hit Seattle in over four decades. We looked down at the city. Sirens blasted and car alarms sang. My daughter and I said nothing. Finally she broke the silence asking, "What stinks?" loud enough to start another earthquake. I looked around the room to throw off suspicion.

"I don't know," I lied, and then slowly headed towards the men's room, where there was a line. I wasn't the only party guilty of incontinence. I left my daughter sitting outside the door and went in and cleaned myself as best I could, disposing of my tainted boxers. They weren't the only pair in the trashcan. When I got back a slow line was proceeding to the elevators. I took my daughter's hand and we filed slowly onto them still in a state of shock.

A half hour later we were looking up at where we'd been, very, very happy to be on the ground. The Space Needle hovered above, unscathed. For forty years of my life it had been a reminder of a day I never wanted to remember. I shunned even looking at it. But now, with my daughter's hand in mine, craning my neck to take in its magnificence and thinking about the tragedy that could have been, I sighed and started to giggle.

My daughter asked. "Can we go back up sometime?"

I looked at her and laughed hysterically. "Are you crazy?" My side hurt from my uncontrollable laughing. She laughed, too. We left, tears welling in our eyes, holding our sides, walking out of the shadow of the Space Needle.

DECEPTION PASS BRIDGE

They had known they would be in town at the same time because of a late-night short-wave telephone call from the Philippines via San Francisco to a New York City operator. Lieutenant Carl Ditmar, "Dit" for short, had used military communications channels, probably illegally, to do nothing more than shoot the shit. He was on a layover in Manila during an Air Force cargo run from California to Australia. All routine except for the six hours he had been spending choking down coffee and listening to the locals gossip in Tagalog. He had been an Air Force pilot for four years, a regular top gun.

Why did he call? To bullshit, of course. He was the king of it. He loved to talk and actually he wasn't a bad listener. The only things that kept them bound were these calls. They had been friends since grade school and had been roommates for three years in college. They were as different as different could be but they would forever be friends.

For the last four years there had been two brief meetings and, in the last two years, nothing but these calls radioed from Kabul, Baghdad, Cuba.

Dit, his bestowed-on-by-Bob nickname, had joined the Air Force and become a pilot as he'd planned. Bob, on the other hand, had traveled to New York on a whim after college, remained in Manhattan in a state of confusion working at odd jobs and painting a little, slowly observing and living the artist's life. He lived in a mammoth Lower East Side apartment. It was over 2500 square feet and he paid nothing for it. Six hundred square feet of it he used as his studio, the rest a center of commerce and amusement for a raggedy bunch of not entirely unsuccessful artists and writers. His art bordered on abstract realism, not yet reaching a true expression of himself. How could it when he still didn't know what himself was?

He had been shown regularly at an almost prestigious gallery. He had sold well and had received some marginal critical acclaim, but still the bucks weren't rolling in (although he was surviving on just his painting and that was an almost impossible feat in New York City). But things weren't all rosy, as he seemed to be stuck in a rut of self-loathing. The art world was going nowhere fast and he felt as if it was being parceled out by the rich and not changing regular people's lives. He felt that was art's purpose: to change people's lives. He still loved to paint, though, and that was what he was doing when Dit called.

"Hello."

"Hey, asshole artist." The voice was familiar but the connection was bad. And his ears echoed of the Train CD playing way too loudly from his stereo. He hit the volume of the remote and let the voice sink in.

"Dit?"

"Who else?"

"Where the hell are you?"

"The Philippines, on a layover, hopefully not for long. I'm waiting for a CIA agent, who is stirring up trouble down here with the Muslim extremists. He's type-A. A for biggest asshole in the world."

"Sounds like fun." Bob tried to picture Dit and the CIA agent.

"Is the rumor true that you're going to be back on the rock at the end of this month?" The rock was Whidbey Island in Washington state, their childhood home.

"September 26th. A long-overdue vacation," Bob confirmed.

"I'm going to be in town."

"Alone?"

"Solo."

"Really?" Bob said, wondering why Dit was coming. His parents no longer lived in town and he was married with a kid. Why would he want to come to a sleepy town where nothing ever happened? There was something in his voice. "Everything all right?"

"Mostly not. And I've been having a dream." Dit stopped, and Bob heard someone in the background. "Oh no, I got to go, Bob. The mole's back and he's jumpy. I'll be in touch."

"Looking forward to it," Bob said, listening to short wire ether, thinking about Dit's dream, and recognizing that something in Dit's voice wasn't altogether right.

He would continue to think about those two things right up to the time they met at the Oak Harbor Tavern.

Many beers, too many stories, and some fairly good drunken pool playing later, Bob and Dit found themselves staring at each other over a pitcher of Olympia Beer. Last call came and they ordered another pitcher and taunted each other, each claiming the right to be called the world's greatest pool player. They were quite convincing when they didn't have a cue in their hand.

"So you're flying the big birds, eh? Killing the innocents in war and all that good stuff?" Bob sloshed, not crossing any lines that had not already been crossed.

Dit grimaced. "We're protecting your sweet artist ass and don't you forget it." Dit drank and played with his cue like it was Chinese self-defense weapon.

"Yeah, USA! USA! USA!" Bob mocked. "We're going to kick some helpless Iraqi butt. God bless America. Mission accomplished." Bob saluted.

"You really are an artist asshole." Dit mocked anger.

"Yes, but an American artist asshole, General. A hungry American artist asshole, General."

"Hungry, huh? I'm hungry, too. Let's go over to George Wong's for some fried rice." Dit leaned against the table, spying the pool balls.

"George isn't amongst the living anymore. His cook

killed him with a cleaver," Bob deadpanned.

"I heard. A cleaver right in the middle of his head. Split his skull like an egg. They sent the cook up the river. He's probably making great Chinese food in the joint."

"Yeah, he was a damn good cook." Bob laughed and Dit joined him. "Now they got some Mexican whipping up all kinds of Chinese delicacies, and they all taste like salsa," Bob rapped.

"Sounds good, let's go," Dit said.

"Yeah, and you can tell me about your trials and tribulations, and about your dream," Bob slurred.

"It's more like a nightmare. A Deception Pass Bridge nightmare," Dit grimaced.

"We all have them," Bob said, resurrecting the common known fact that all the kids that lived in Oak Harbor and ever went to the bridge would sooner or later have a nightmare about falling off of it.

"It's not about falling, or maybe it is. It's you and I walking across Deception Pass Bridge. Actually we're walking underneath it, on the girders," Dit explained.

"Yeah?" Bob flinched, not wanting to go there.

"You did it once didn't you, Bob? You told me you did?"

Bob knew that was coming. "Kinda," he answered, still haunted by the lie.

"Kinda? You don't kinda walk under Deception Pass Bridge."

"I did. I mean I did. Let's go eat," Bob said, standing, trying to escape the subject. They stumbled out into the damp island air, zipping up their coats, blowing breath clouds and jamming their hands into their pockets. George Wong's was across Pioneer Boulevard. They jaywalked, a bit wobbly.

"Drunk?" Dit asked.

"Yep."

They walked into George Wong's, the smell of soy sauce enveloping them. They sat down at the first empty booth. It was lit by a small lamp that had a Johnny Walker Black shade. They looked at each other and listened to the people around them. There weren't that many but the few that were there were loud.

"In my dream we never make it across the bridge the whole way," Dit continued like he never stopped.

"What happens?"

"I wake up."

"You wake up?" Bob cracked his neck.

"Yeah."

"What'll you have, boys?" the waitress interrupted standing above them. She was dark-haired, fifty, cake make-up that even in the darkness could not cover her drawn, weary face. At some point in her life she had drunk heavily, aging herself before her time.

"I'll have an order of pork fried rice and a side of ribs and a Bud." Bob smiled.

"Same." Dit nodded.

"Thank you." The waitress smiled and left them alone.

"Hasn't changed a bit," Dit laughed, looking around.

"The only thing missing is old George cussing the cook."

"Yep."

"I miss George," Dit sighed.

"Don't go emotional on me. It's not becoming of a military man."

"I know. It's just, shit fuck."

"'Shit fuck'!" Bob laughed, "'Shit fuck'? First it's dreams about walking under bridges; now it's shit fuck. I mean, Dit, what the fuck is shit fuck?" Bob laughed harder and Dit joined him, the slight tension of an oncoming confession being broken.

"It's my life, it's my wife, and it's the military. It's all getting a little tense and crazy."

"Why wouldn't it be? We're at war with half the world and you're flying into it and through it," Bob said seriously.

"I'm trying to fly around it." Dit laughed. "Nobody knows what we're doing."

"The neo-cons do." Bob groaned, not wanting to get into politics. "I gotta tell you, I think the war is a sham. I mean, I was in Manhattan when the towers fell. I had two friends who died in them. I tasted the dust of the annihilation. But there was no one from Iraq flying those planes. We're killing people because we can."

"I'm not disagreeing." Dit silenced the onslaught of an argument and then continued. "It's strange, since I've been having this dream I've been thinking a lot about Deception Pass Bridge. What a great name. I mean, when you go over that bridge and leave this island, beware of the deception; it's everywhere. There couldn't be a better name for that bridge."

The waitress interrupted the diatribe, putting four plates and two beers onto the table. This was followed by a nourishing silence as they went to work on the food and drank the beer.

Then Dit started talking about the dream. It started with them walking under the bridge on the girdered arch. He led Bob to the top of the arch and then something happened. It was terrifying but he could not remember it. The last thing he remembered was looking back at Bob. No matter how hard he would try to stay asleep and continue the dream, he could not. He had been having the dream once a week for the last two months. It was becoming an obsession.

Bob listened curiously, having the feeling of where this was going. Bob never did walk under the bridge. It was a dare that led him to lie. He was a junior in high school when he went out to the bridge, alone, inched his way underneath to the huge iron girders, climbed up and onto them, looked down at the swirling waters … and chickened out. But he'd told everyone he had actually done it. And now it was ten years later, back to haunt him.

"What time is it?" Dit asked, throwing a gnawed rib onto his plate.

"Two," Bob answered, looking back at the neon-lit clock above the kitchen door.

"What do you say we get some beer and go out to the bridge?" Dit said, staring at Bob.

"I'm not climbing under it. That's suicide." And it was. Many a suicide had been committed jumping off the bridge. If you jumped or fell, hitting the water at one hundred miles an hour was like hitting cement, and if the fall didn't kill you you'd drown in the swift currents and frigid water. No one had ever survived.

"You think I'm crazy," Dit said, and he laughed. "I'm more afraid of that than anything. Let's just go bullshit and watch the sunrise."

"Bullshit at the bridge?" Bob laughed. "Why not?"

They paid their bill and headed out. Deception Pass Bridge connected Whidbey Island to Fidalgo Island. The most beautiful place in the world, some people might say. It was an awesome sight. It was actually two bridges spanning a glacier-cut pass of stone. The longest span ran from Whidbey Island to Pass Island, the shorter from Pass Island to Fidalgo Island. Pass Island stood in the middle of the waterway channeling the water into two passes, Deception Pass and Canoe Pass. From the bridge to the water it was 182 feet, surrounded by evergreen trees and sheer cliffs and punctuated with an occasional bald eagle soaring beneath. Looking down to see eagles soaring. That was a trip. Deception Pass was discovered by Captain George Vancouver, who thought the Pass might be the Northwest Passage, but instead found it to be a deception, so the story goes. Thus the name.

In the lot next to the bridge, Dit and Bob parked their car and sat drinking beer and chewing on beef jerky.

"So New York is okay, huh?" Dit asked.

"Yeah. Besides being on orange alert twenty-four hours a day and the economy sucking wind, it's all right," Bob sighed.

"What's the women situation?"

"Let's see, I'm seeing three women. One is an actress, who spends most of her time in a deep funk because of her miserable life; another is an advertising account executive who has the same miserable life and funk; and the third is a nurse, who, coincidently, has the same miserable life and same deep funk, but at least she gives a great massage. So I find myself in a constant deep funk with an occasional massage. It's a lot of fun. How about you? Jeannie? Hannah?" Bob asked, knowing there was reason for concern.

"I'm never there. It's rough. I think Jeannie would leave me if she had another option. She is with her mom now pow-wowing on how to proceed. At least that's what I infer."

"Tough. What's going to happen?"

"Don't know? The world's got to change. I might opt out and try to snag a job with an airline."

"Wow. That's big. No more military?"

"I don't love the military anymore. I love flying. It's not that the Air Force is bad. It's that it's ... I don't know, it's like riding a huge prehistoric dinosaur. You don't go anywhere because you're already extinct."

"And what do you suggest?" Bob asked, falling back into

148

the rap with Dit so comfortably. Effortless talk, as though they'd never been apart. Bullshit.

"Well you know I have thought on this subject."

"I bet you have." Bob chuckled.

"Our military is obsolete."

"It is? I thought that it was fighting wars on two fronts and winning. At least that's what Dubya tells us," Bob joked.

Dit grimaced. "The only war that matters is the one against terrorism, and we're losing it. How you fight terrorism is with swift, strong retaliation by a very efficient task force."

"Yeah, but couldn't we try some peace, love and understanding first?" Bob sighed.

"What I want is an apolitical force, something created through the United Nations, a sort of French Foreign Legion, the baddest and best. And whoever should dare pull a terrorist action would have to deal with the wrath of this force."

"Is that all?" Bob smiled.

"There is one other thing." Dit sipped on his beer.

"What's that?"

"I think I'm the man for the job."

"Okay, General."

"As you were."

"Thank you, sir." Bob saluted. "What will be your first order?"

"Drink the rest of this beer." Dit smiled.

They drank and conversed for hours. Dit would turn the car on for heat and defrost to rid the car of the hot air that was sticking to the windows. After consuming the half case of beer, they fell out of the car to stretch and relieve themselves. The air sobered them. The sky was lit on the eastern horizon in back of the Cascade Mountains. Dawn was coming.

Dit headed down a trail and Bob followed, feeling uncomfortable, knowing where they were going. Together they stood in front of the mammoth cement block that was the beginning of the span of Deception Pass Bridge. The girders were massive beams with intermeshed supporting steel criss-crossing from beam to beam creating a walkway that formed the arch that spanned the waterway from island to island. Huge iron support beams ran at forty-five-degree angles from the span to the road and bridge. The bolts welded into the beams and arches holding it all together were as big as manhole covers. The two friends looked up at the iron works of the bridge and were dwarfed by it.

"I gotta do this," Dit said, starting the climb up. He stood on the vault and reached out for the mammoth iron beam. He pulled himself to the span the width of a sidewalk that arched up. He began to walk it, holding onto the vertical beams.

"You're crazy!" Bob screamed, getting sober.

"Maybe. Shit, George Wong is dead, cleaver in the head. I hate my job. My wife and kid don't know me. The world sucks, and I'm having this nightmare that's driving me bonkers. I guess you're right. I am crazy."

"Yes, you are! Don't do it!" Bob pleaded, "I have to tell you something."

"What?" Dit stopped and looked down.

"I lied." Bob confessed.

"You son of a bitch! Now you've gotta get up here. You got something to prove, too. Lied? Shit fuck. So you've gotta get rid of the demons, Bob. Come on. We'll watch the sunrise from the middle."

"No."

"Fine. So fuck you. I'll be back." Dit started his climb.

Bob stood staring for a minute, kicked the ground and began to climb. His pride carried him. "Wait!"

"Nope. Catch me," Dit yelled.

Bob followed nervously, hugging beams and praying as he went. He looked up to watch Dit climbing steadily, nearing the top of the arch.

"Look!" Dit yelled and pointed at the rising sun.

Bob looked at the sun and then looked back up at Dit, who was skirting around the last beam connection before the downward side of the arch. As he watched him, he thought Dit was being over-confident, careless. "Dit!" he called. Dit seemed to wave at him, as though everything was fine, but then, like that, Dit lost his balance and disappeared from Bob's view.

"Dit!" Bob yelled in disbelief. "Dit!!"

There was no answer.

Bob panicked. He could not see him. Forgetting the precariousness of the climb, he hurried on fearlessly around the beam connections. There was Dit, alive, hanging upside down by his right foot that was wedged in a joining of two beams. He was silent, frozen by fear.

Bob moved toward the stuck foot and Dit's hanging body.

"Shit! You dumb shit." Bob swore, looking at the wedged foot, his heart pounding. He braced his legs against the iron girder, wedging them. He leaned over and looked at the Pass running far below and Dit frozen in midair. Everything seemed to be moving in slow motion.

"Dit, you've got to pull yourself up so I can grab your arms."

"My ankle?"

"It's wedged pretty good. It will hurt but you've got to do it."

"Okay," Dit answered and raised his hands and Bob grabbed them and pulled him up. Dit groaned from the pressure on his ankle. When Bob got him back on the beam Dit's shoe twisted loose and fell from his foot to the water below. The splash was imperceptible from where they sat.

"My Nike."

"Your Nike? How about your life! My life!" Bob began to cry uncontrollably.

"You saved my life!" Dit began to cry, too. They sat on the girder and hugged each other, consoling themselves. Sobbing, they watched the rising sun brighten the world, lighting up all in front of them. They marveled at it, and at themselves, and they talked awhile longer in quiet hushed tones that sounded like prayer.